THE

Secrets

WE KEEP

2

A NOVEL BY

BRITT JONI

DEDICATION

.

Dorothy, Bobby, and J.C. this one is for you!
May you all rest beautifully in peace!

ACKNOWLEDGMENTS

Buddha: Thanks for being so understanding when Mommy was up so many late nights and encouraging me with your smile when I felt like giving up. You are EVERYTHING, my love, and don't you forget it. I love you more than most. Shoot for the stars, and reach the moon.

Mommy: YOU ARE THE TRUTH! THANK YOU FOR THE COUNTLESS THINGS YOU DO! You've been my voice of reason and my pillar of strength on days when I'm unsure of what God is trying to tell me and where He is leading me to go.

To my Big girls: Mama Britt loves y'all. You've made these last ten years so sweet. But you can't read this book until you're thirty. Lol.

Jil: Thank you for kicking me in gear and encouraging me to follow my dreams. Thanks for taking the time to read when no one else would and keeping it a secret. Thanks for being a stickler in me practicing good time management. I could never repay you for the strength you poured into me to do this.

Ernyka: My Jess the Mess, thanks for holding me accountable and reminding me that I do truly have a gift. You went hard for me to finish this, and I appreciate it.

Quiana: Ooooowee, Q. Where do I start? You are so supportive and loving. You have allowed so many dreamers to spread their wings.

You push me when I need to be pushed, but you also allow me to be authentically me. Thank you for believing in me and calming my nerves during the process of completing this novel. You could never begin to understand the magnitude of how much I appreciate you taking a chance on me. Because of you, I'm learning to trust the process.

MKP Fam: I am amazed at all the talent I see in our group, and I am so honored to be amongst such great authors/people. I found family behind our dope ass pens.

To my family and friends: I love y'all! This year started off rough, but by the grace of God, we are still standing. When people say they don't have a supportive group of people behind them, I honestly don't know what that feels like, because y'all ride for "Shooter" like nobody's business.

Judi P, Coke, & Sherricka B.: Surprised to see your names listed, huh? Lol. You two are the real MVPs. You two allowed me to see that, in this industry, my work is appreciated. You motivated me to complete this novel. THANKS.

To my Test/Beta readers: You all came through in the clutch. When I say you all made me work for this novel here. You saw my soul and continuously pushed me to be a better writer. I thank you all for helping me on my journey!

britt joni
-PENNING LOVE NATURALLY-

A NOTE TO MY READERS

Hey, Love Muffin!

First, if you are reading this page, I thank you. I thank you for taking a chance on a new author. I hope to be one that you enjoy and that you give me a chance to enter your heart for a while. Like most of you, I am an avid reader myself, so I will get your frustration with me. But bear with me, for I am human. Although I welcome all constructive criticism, please allow me the chance to process it before I respond, for I am a thinker. I love writing, so know that I am actively working to be a better writer for the both of us. I will say that if you're looking for a novel with a reformed thug or a man strictly from the streets, this is not the novel for you. Will I eventually write one? Who knows? I'll follow wherever my pen leads me. I hope you enjoy this sequel as much as I enjoyed writing it. Please leave an honest review. I would greatly and graciously appreciate it.

Britt Joni.

PREVIOUSLY ...

Kwame

It's been a few days since I've laid eyes on Gaea, and although I still feel some type of way, I can't help but miss her. She has only been in my space for a few days, but it seems as if her scent is embedded into every crevice of my home. The more I lie in this bed, the more the sweet smell of sunflowers tickles my nose. It's in my sheets and my pillows—hell, even in the T-shirt I'm wearing. It seems as if no matter what my housekeeper does, there's no getting her scent out of my home. Not that I want it to go anywhere; the shit is just annoying, knowing that I can't have her right now. I can't begin to understand and sympathize with her when my baby girl is gone. Like the shit doesn't involve rocket science. Why can't she see that Aaron is behind the disappearance of Kynsley?

I have worked it all out in my head, and no matter how I flip shit, it always comes to Aaron. It makes perfect sense. He's always lurking in the shadows of Gaea and Kynsley. Kurt, a member of my security team, made sure to let me know he had been snooping around their neighborhood. I want so bad to continue being mad at her, but how can I honestly be? She isn't privy to that type of information, so she can't possibly know that this nigga is completely out of his mind like he's dove head first into a cesspool of crazy. I don't see the connection that makes him believe that my baby girl is his. Like the nigga is full-blown light-skinned, and my baby is kissed by chocolate. Like, nothing is making sense.

I jump out of bed and catch a shower before I go over to my mom's to check in on her and my sister. As I'm waiting for my breakfast, my mind shifts to Janet. While I have been in constant communication with Theodore, I can't begin to pretend to stomach her. Something isn't sitting well within my soul when it comes to her. Yeah, she adores Kynsley, but her smug looks are a bit too condescending. I don't think she will harm her; I just think her care and love—or lack thereof—is disingenuous.

If I'm being honest with myself, that is part of the reason Gaea and I connect on the level in which we do. The two people that are supposed to love and care for us and show us what unconditional love is, they failed us. They give us our first heartbreaks that ultimately turn into scars, pushing us to a place where we crave love rather than healing. We're two broken souls, searching for healing in each other.

Once I knew for sure that Kynsley was mine, I made a vow to myself that she would never feel that type of pain. No kid deserves to go through life and search for the love of a parent. I make sure she feels the depth of my love in every ounce of any time we spend together. I put in not only my money but also my time because that's what she needs most. Knowing that she's missing when I never truly got the chance to be a father is crippling, and to top the shit off, Gaea is being so fucking stubborn. Once I have them both back in my life, I'm going to make it my life's mission to ensure that they're not only safe but also that Gaea knows what the fuck is up. I've had enough of her running when shit gets tough.

Armed with that feeling, I get out of bed, shower, and head toward my kitchen. Imagine my surprise when Tobias is not only in my home but also in my kitchen, eating my lunch. I'm not in the mood for his lectures today, but having someone around eases the sting of my girls not being with me.

"Hey, Kwame, I got a text earlier from Gaea asking me to check out a Lisette Toussaint, and you may want to take a look at this," Tobias says, interrupting my thoughts.

"Aww, for real?" I ask, not really caring one way or another what the hell they were talking about. I try to play it cool, but I'm madder than a muthafucka. She's talking to every damn body in our circle but the one person she needs to talk to. I'm not with this passive aggressive shit, letting others know about shit before me. Hell, I'm her man. Well, am I? Man, fuck that. Ain't no guessing; I am her man.

"Stop being that way. You know you love the girl. She's just well... Simply put, she's Ana's sister."

"Ana's sister, huh? What's up with y'all anyway? Don't think I forgot about y'all coming back into the studio all discombobulated," I say, giving a half chuckle.

"Nothing. Mind ya business," he says, completely dismissing me. "But yo, I need you to take a look at what I found."

I walk over to take a look at his screen, and I'm completely shocked at what I see. There is no way we could've missed this shit. I immediately pick up my phone and dial Theodore.

"Hey, Pops, I need you to check something out," I blurt out.

"Are you speaking about this Lisette Toussaint that Gaea sent over?" he asks. "I have a file about two inches thick, but I haven't been able to look at it quite yet."

"We went to undergrad with her. But I don't see how she would connect with Kynsley."

"Hmm..." he says while shuffling through some papers. "It looks as if the connection just so happens to be none other than Aaron W. Williamson."

Gaea's dad, Tobias, and I decide that instead of having this conversation over the phone, it will be best if we have this conversation face to face. We agree upon a time to meet, but I also decide that with recent events, despite how pissed off I am at Gaea, I need her safe. I've been kicking myself ever since I walked out the door on her. It was childish, but my feelings were 100 percent valid. Yes, I understand her viewpoint on Maxwell being a suspect, but she isn't even willing to explore the possibility that there are other avenues. Hell, that's my father, and while I don't want to believe it, I threw his ass in the list of people to look out for. Why? Because the love of my daughter won't allow me to just let anyone to be overlooked. If I thought it was my mother, I would have thrown her in the list of people I thought wanted to hurt Kynsley.

Armed with this information, I make my way over to Gaea's house to sit down and have an actual conversation—one that requires us to put our differences aside and to focus on facts rather than emotions. While I love this woman, it's her stubbornness that I can only stomach in small doses. I can't shake this spine-chilling feeling as I turn to get on the off ramp toward her house. Not wanting to alert Pops on just a feeling, I call Tobias up and ask him, along with security, to meet me at the house.

As I pull into her driveway, nothing appears to be out of place. Her purple Jeep Wrangler Sahara sits in her driveway as normal, and her landscaping looks beautiful, as it always has. But once I get to the door, my heart drops into my stomach. The bright-yellow door is left slightly ajar. I don't get a good feeling by the door being open. She never leaves doors open despite her living in a gated community. Sensing she may be in some kind of trouble, I forego waiting on security and calling the police. I rush into the house with wild abandon, searching the house and frantically calling out to her. By the time I make it to her bedroom, I hear footsteps and more voices. I take it as my cue that security and the police Tobias called have finally made it.

I enter her bedroom and feel a sense of relief when I see her curled in bed, fast asleep. She looks so peaceful and angelic at that moment that I don't want to disturb her. At this moment, I know I can't live without her. But I won't reveal that fact to her until I know she is on the same page as me romantically, physically, and spiritually. I'm not in the space to properly deal with my feelings, and she's definitely not in the space to accept what I have to offer her. I gently stir her to get her to open those eyes I've come to love.

"Hey, Gypsy. Wake up, baby," I speak gently, and she starts to move. She looks shocked to see me as she opens her eyes. Then I see a flicker in her eyes and know that whatever is about to come out of her mouth is about to be some straight bullshit. But I'd rather hear that than to not hear anything at all. Her time to tame that mouth will soon come; of that, I'm sure.

"I see showing up unannounced seems to be a strong point of yours. But let me also add breaking and entering to that list," she says, rolling her eyes and moving out of my grasp. I make a choice to ignore her stubborn ass. Now knowing that she's safe, I start to move around the room, packing her bags.

"I didn't break in, Gaea. The door was open. Get out of the bed and start helping me to pack these bags so we can go. Better yet, throw some clothes on, and I'll pay someone to come pack up the house."

"Have you lost your mind? My door was closed. I made sure I locked up and set the alarm prior to lying down for a nap. Furthermore, I am not giving up my house to live with you."

"First, you have no choice in the matter anymore. The door was not only unlocked, but it was also opened. But your so-called alarm system was disarmed. Now get up willingly, or be moved forcefully," I declare. Getting the feeling that I'm dead serious, she gets up and collects her things. Once she's gathered most of the things she thinks she'll need, we make our way to the door.

"Aye, Flash, I need you to come check something out," Kion, the head of my security, says, and the look on his face lets me know it's something he doesn't want Gaea to see. I instruct Tobias to stay put with Gaea until I check out what they've found. She objects and follows me despite my better judgment. It seems like a lifetime flashes amongst us before we make the trek to Kynsley's room.

I make the decision to open the door and immediately regret the choice. Gaea let's out a gut-wrenching scream as I lose the contents of my stomach on the floor. The room is completely destroyed. The curtains are ripped down. Toys are broken, and a ripped picture of

Kynsley and Gaea has a knife with a snake attached to it stuck in the wall. But what gets me is a filthy image of my baby on the bed.

Smeared across her wall is a bloody message:

YOU RUINED MY LIFE THREE YEARS AGO AND FOR THAT YOU MUST PAY! CALL OFF THE COPS OR SIX FEET UNDER SHALL YOUR DAUGHTER LAY!

CHAPTER 1

Kwame

*H*elpless. I never thought that would be synonymous and coincide with my name. All this time, I've been blinded to believe I was invincible on and off the field. Hell, I'm always a hot topic on ESPN, I beast on the field, and I dominate financially with all of the sponsors I've acquired, yet when it comes down to protecting, better yet finding my baby, I'm at a complete standstill. A man like me can't function, knowing that something that's supposed to be innate, I'm failing at.

It feels as if I'm tucking my tail between my legs for the sake of an image. Well, sort of anyway. I have a few things in play to get the answers I need. I've been holding back for the longest, keeping quiet about a lot of shit, but now this shit was personal. Once I see the blood smeared over my daughter's room, it wakes up a different side of me. This idle sitting shit isn't working for me any longer. I'll be less than the man I already feel I am if I continue to watch the police pussyfoot around while my baby's blood is on my hands. Literally.

I cleaned those walls myself because I needed everything I felt while I washed my baby's blood off those walls to sink in so that once I got my hands on the person I feel is responsible, they'll feel my wrath. It takes everything in me not to act a damn fool and risk everything I've held sacred. The real gut punch was seeing Gaea break down, and hell, if I'm being completely transparent, it enraged me.

That's the only logical reason I can explain currently sitting in Aaron's living room. Everyone's telling me to lay low, but they can tell me that shit until they're blue in the face. I don't give a fuck about my career. The more I still smell the blood of my daughter on my fingers, the angrier I get. For that sole purpose, someone's going to pay for this shit. I don't know how people don't comprehend my pain. But who would? People are often blind to seeing your shit when it isn't directly affecting them. This is my promise missing and more than likely hurt, and I'm watching my earth sink and succumb to her pain.

The more I sit here, waiting for Aaron to show up, the more my irritation grows. This nigga's house is disgusting. You would think with him having a little bit of money, he would hire a maid or something. From the looks of my surroundings, this is barely a step up from a trap house. To think he is actually raising his daughter in this filth.

"Dad, just give me a little more time. Everything with Gaea is falling into place. Granted, it's taken three years of time I can't get back, but nonetheless, we are back on track with her becoming my wife. Give me a few more days, and I'll check back in with a more realistic wedding date. Aight, later, Pops," he says while disconnecting the phone call. I silently watch him walk through his living room, muttering under his breath, never bothering to flip a switch.

I don't know what the fuck is going through that nigga's head, but one thing is clear; he's looney. His reality has to be warped if he even thinks for one minute that Gaea will be anything other than a past lover of his. As he continues to mumble a bunch of nothing, I follow him with my eyes as he finally flips a switch, and I chuckle at the shocked expression on his face to find me sitting on his nasty ass couch.

"What the fuck are you doing in my house, nigga?" he asks while making his way toward me. The click of my gun stops him dead in his tracks.

"You were always one to never pay attention to your surroundings," I state.

"Nigga, have you lost your fucking mind, coming up in my spot with this incognegro shit?" he snarls out.

"That's the wrong question to ask, my nigga! The better question is, where the fuck is my daughter?"

"Man, you mean my daughter? Clearly, yo' ass must be lost in Gaea's pussy, because there is no way in hell you don't see what I see. If Janet hadn't confirmed it, it would still be clear as fucking day she belongs to me."

"Listen, man, I don't have time to listen to you talk about shit that makes no fucking sense. I just need you to tell me where Kynsley is before I put a bullet in yo' ass," I growl out, not letting that Janet comment escape me.

"Don't threaten me in my—" he begins to say as the round I send into him causes his body to spurt out blood. "Shit! Oh my God, this shit burns!"

"Fuck all that! Answer the question, and I'll get you some help!" I spit out after I readjust the silencer on my gun. Meanwhile, he's hopping around like a little bitch. I glance out his window to see his mother and daughter are pulling up. I quickly turn and make a beeline toward him, cursing myself for not planning better. I signal my bodyguard Kion to get him out of the house as quickly and quietly as possible. Since it's taking her a while to get Sidney out of the car, I take that as my opportunity to get the fuck out of dodge while my men stay behind to get the blood out of the way. Lucky for us, baby girl is throwing a tantrum with her grandmother. I sprint out the back to a blacked-out suburban. Once in the vehicle, I take Aaron's phone. "I'm calling your mother. If you know what's best, you'll tell her you had to run out of town to handle some last-minute business."

"Bullshit! She won't believe it!" he snarls.

"Make it believable then," I say while placing the barrel of the gun to his head and the phone on speaker.

"Hey, Ma! Can you watch Sid for a few days? I have to run out of town to handle some stuff!"

"Aaron, you sure know how to make my asshole itch! I'll keep her, but I swear to God if you're out chasing that bitch again, I'll kill you," she says before she disconnects the call.

We drive for a total of thirty minutes before we pull up to my cabin. At this point, Aaron is starting to look a little weak and is sweating profusely, so I check to make sure that my on-call physician is in place before we exit the vehicle. I honestly have no intentions of killing him; I just need to scare him enough so that he'll give up information in regard to the whereabouts of my child. It's obvious at this point that he can't possibly know anything about my baby girl's whereabouts. He's just as clueless as I am about her. All this time, I've been hyper-focused on him when it seems my focus should've been on Janet's trifling ass. Her duck ass knows that Aaron isn't the father of Kynsley, but she planted that little seed of certainty in his head.

"Look, man, I'm going to get someone to check you out. I'm not sorry for doing the shit, because I still don't have the answers I need. With all of that being said, I'm not trying to kill you."

"So you mean to tell me this shit ain't a publicity stunt, and my daughter is really missing?" Aaron slurs.

"I don't know what Janet's aim was in telling you that Kynsley is yours, but she is definitely my kid. Even if paternity wasn't established, just by glancing at her, Aaron, you have to know that there is no possibility she is yours," I state.

"She does look like you, I'll admit, but Janet and my mom assured me that she was mine. They told me that Gaea was just caught up on a feeling with you and that she'd eventually stop being mad at me. From what I gathered, she is still very much in love with me. She's just mad."

"I can't verify her feelings for you one way or the other. All that I can say for certain is that Kynsley is most definitely mine. So understand it's imperative that I know any information that you have," I say, knowing that I can tell him how Gaea feels, I just don't feel like hearing the shit he'll have to say in response. It's clear as day that whatever Janet and Aaron's mother have concocted is embedded in his brain. I can't change it, but I can utilize his naivety to my benefit.

CHAPTER 2

Gaea

*M*ost people think I'm insane for continuing to work while my daughter's missing, but honestly, it's the only thing keeping me sane. I just need to do something to drown out the guilt of not being present at the moment when she was snatched. I can't stand to look at Kwame in the face without being angry. I know it isn't his fault, but had I not been so wrapped in him, I believe I would be holding my baby in my arms. So for now, to clear my head, I've been picking up shifts and pushing myself to strive harder to forget the pain I'm going through. Even if that means I'm not getting the rest that I should be getting.

"Gaea, I get wanting to keep busy love, but as not only your friend, but as your supervisor, I can't allow you to pick up any more shifts," Jenn says as she sits down to watch me complete my charts.

"Jenn, I'm fine. I can handle it. Plus, you need the help. We are already running short," I pleaded with her.

"Butterfly, I can't do that. You're running from your problems, and I can't allow that. I need your head here, baby, and right now, you can't give me that. Do I trust that you're going to give your patients the best care possible? Yes. But you aren't being fair to yourself to continue down this path. Take a few days and then come back to me fresh," Jenn says while rubbing my trembling hands.

"There will be no need for you to return, Ms. Lee. You are being terminated effective immediately."

I turn my head, looking into the face of the beautiful woman I encountered a couple weeks back. I can't place her from my past, so I don't understand the need for her to be so hostile toward me. "Excuse me? What?" I mumble.

"No need to get hostile. Your services are just no longer needed. No harsh feelings, love!" she coos.

"On what grounds, Lisette? We are already running short," Jenn says.

"On the grounds that this is an at-will company, and I don't like her ass," she spits out.

"Wah di hell! Di gyal ave lose har mind!" Jenn spits out, clearly pissed to the highest point of pissedivity to start speaking Jamaican Patois.

"What? I don't even know you!" I spit out.

"Humph! Sure you don't, and now you won't get the chance to figure out how you know me. You have fifteen minutes to collect your things and vacate the premises. Jenn, we will call an agency to cover all of your staffing needs!"

"Dis a crazy! Dis gyal ave shit fi brains. A jealous heart is a dangerous thing," Jenn continues on.

"I just don't understand!" I stutter out, clearly confused by what just happened.

She lets out a menacing laugh before she says, "I'm sure if you fuck Kwame just right, he'd take care of you!"

"Oh, so this is what is this huh? That little pussy mad because the dick that she wants doesn't want her! Hmm. It's a sad thing really. If I didn't give a fuck about my license, I would drag your ass all up and through this hospital. Lucky for the both of us, I do. Consider yourself blessed. Furthermore, I don't need Kwame or anyone to take care of me. I take care of myself and my daughter! Before, during, and after a

7

man! I'm a self-made bitch! The next time you think to approach a bitch about a man you want, word to the wise, don't do it with me! I'm not the fucking one!" I state.

"You got all that mouth but have yet to locate said daughter with your extra pathetic ass!"

Before I know what's happening I have that bitch by her throat and I am banging her head against the nurse's station. I'm two piecing her ass so good that it takes about three male nurses to pull me off of her. I don't know what her deal is, but it's obvious that she and Kwame may have had some dealings. Today, she chose to fuck with the right one, and I'm going to be the very one to set her ass straight. I keep cool and I never bother anybody, but here she comes with the shits. All of my pent up frustrations were coming out and it wasn't looking pretty for her. Right when I'm about to stomp her face in, Kion comes to grab me. As they pick us both up, I kick her dead in her face so hard it breaks her nose.

"No, boss lady. I can't have you up here carrying on like this! Yo, Miguel, get Ms. Lee to the car while I handle this shit up here."

As Miguel tosses me over his shoulder, I call out for Jenn to call me once her shift ends. As soon as we get to the car, I start blowing Kwame's phone up. There's no way in the world he's hiding a whole bitch from me while he has me living in his home. This isn't the Kwame I know. This shit is messy, and I can't stomach that, like, at all.

It takes us all of thirty minutes to drive home, and just as soon as he puts the car in park, I jump out and check the garage to make sure his stupid ass is at home. Seeing his car, I sprint up the stairs and kick the bathroom door open. All the words I need to say are caught in my throat as I stand and stare at Kwame's body in amazement. Leave it to my dick-deprived ass to let the argument slip from my lips when I have perfection staring me right in the face. *Down, girl. Check his ass.*

"Gaea, what the fuck is wrong with you, kicking down doors and shit?"

I can't even answer his ass, because my panties are now soaked. I approach and free him from his towel. I drop to my knees and pull his mushroom head into my mouth while gently stroking his balls. I run my tongue along his length before I make his thick, veiny dick disappear down my throat. While keeping him deep in my throat, I get rid of my pants and start playing with my pussy.

"Shit, Gaea! Why didn't you say anything? Is this what you wanted?" Kwame asks while gently fucking my mouth. Fully lost in the moment, I pull my mouth off of his dick to start pumping away and gently suckling on his balls. I increase the speed of my pumps and feel his dick twitch, signaling he's about to reach his peak. Just as he's about to cum, I latch on to his penis, sucking sloppily for dear life as he releases his delicious seeds down my throat, and I greedily swallow it all, quickening my pace with my fingers strumming on my clitoris. My fingers are quickly replaced with his thick tongue. I push my pussy deeper into his face. He begins to lick up one side, over the top of my clit, flattening his tongue, then back down the other side. He did that a few times and then began to openly fuck me with his tongue.

"I don't want you to cum just yet," he says, yanking me up and gently squeezing my throat and entering me roughly.

"Ah shit, baby!" I cry out.

"So why the fuck did you kick the door in, Gaea?" he asks while working his hips, pushing his luscious dick in and out of me.

"Ahhhh, that's not important right now! Just fuck me, daddy!"

"Nah, Gypsy, talk to me," he says while increasing his speed and tapping on my G-spot.

"Shit, daddy, just like that! Fuck me harder!" I moan out.

"Hold on to the sink, Gaea. If you let it go, I won't let you nut. If you lose your arch, I won't let you nut. Understand, I'm gonna get mine off the strength of you kicking down a door that was unlocked!" he growled into my ear, and I got wetter. Kwame began drilling into my pussy like his life depended on it. The faster he stroked, the more my stress was placed in the back of my head. For a moment I was taken back to the very first night we made love.

"No, Kwame, I want you. I need you now."

"I'm not sure you're ready for that, babe. I can see you're hurting, and I don't want this to be something you live to regret."

"Kwame, please don't deny me. I need you to help me to take the pain away," I say as I step out of my panties.

"Gaea, I don't—" Before he can get his sentence out, I've climbed onto his lap, silencing him with an electrifying kiss.

He tried his hardest to resist the urge, but unfortunately, it's a losing battle. He pulls back. "Babe, once we cross this line, I want you to be aware that there is no turning back. I need you to understand the ramifications of what we are about to do."

"Darling, I've never been surer about anything in my life."

He swallows his better judgement and give into flesh despite his spirit telling him to go in the opposite direction. He feels it in his gut that nothing will be the same after this, but still he can't stop himself. His spirit is screaming at him to feed my soul and to speak to and stroke my bleeding heart. But how can he explain to me that his soul has this innately deep desire to heal my soul, even if it's only temporary, without freaking me out. He knows no other way to do this than to be completely open and direct.

"Gaea Lee, look at me," he says so that I could look up, see, and under-stand how serious he am. When he's sure my almond-hazel eyes meet mine, he continues. "I can give you all of the physical pleasure your heart could ever possibly desire, but right now, in this here moment, I'm going to take my time and caress your soul and make love to your heart. If you're not prepared for that, I need you to speak up now." I see a look of confusion play across her face, so I continued. "If I can't do those things for you, then we can't continue. You're important to me, Gypsy, so if I'm going to take care of you, I have to start with your heart."

I glance back up at him and croak out, "Just stop talking and do whatever it is you need to do,"

"God, you're beautiful," he says as he leans over to kiss me deeply, passionately. He draws his body against me and grasp me firmly. He traces kisses along my ears, down my neck, then down my arm, and speaks softly into my ear. "I'm not just talking about the things that the world can see; I'm speaking of the inner you. The beauty of your spirit beguiles me, the stillness of your soul arouses me, and the quiet strength of your heart enthuses me."

He drops his hands down to reach under the hem of my dress and slide it along my thigh. Slowly, he moves it higher and higher along my smooth skin.

The edge of his hand feels the heat first, then the baldness of my sweet spot, and finally the wet oasis of my pussy. I close my eyes gasp, and my legs spread wider as I push my pussy against his hand. Seeing the pleasure play all over my face, he turns his hand ninety degrees and gently run his middle finger up and down my clitoris. Kwame slowly pushes his finger into my canal and I feel my breath catch. I smile a devious smile as he eases his finger in and out of me. Right when he can feel I'm at my peak, he removes his fingers. He puts his fingers into my mouth so I can taste myself and whisper against my lips, "You are intelligent, you are beautiful, and you are more than worthy to be loved.".

As he spills his seeds in me, I realize what a grand mistake I've made. When things go wrong, I run to Kwame and force him to make it better. I never face my real issues. I let him dick me down into submission and I continue on like nothing ever happened. Well, not today. He's about to get this mouth and then some.

We both shower silently as I begin brooding about the events of today.

"I lost my job today," I mumble as Kwame pulls me into his arms and placed a chaste kiss on the back of my neck.

"I'm sorry to hear that, baby. You don't need that job anyway," he mutters.

"Funny you should say that. I had an interesting encounter with Lisette Toussaint. I was fired and told if I fucked you right, you would take care of me." I feel his body stiffen before he gives off a nervous chuckle.

"I mean, where is the lie here?"

"Bae, I mean, *Flash*, stop fucking playing with me. I had to beat that bitch ass today. Speaking of, you may want to talk to Kion."

"I mean, you out here beating bitches up, and I shot Aaron… Shit…" he mutters. "Look, go to sleep while I go and talk with Kion."

"Nah, nigga, get back over here and tell me what the fuck you talking about."

"Nigga? I'm gonna let that shit slide because you in yo' feelings, but don't get beside yourself. Watch how you talk to me," he says.

"You act like you're my man or something."

"Because I am. Now shut the hell up and go to sleep," he says before disappearing out of the door.

I kept tossing around with sleep evading me, so I do what I do best. I get out of bed and find my keyboard in one of the guest bedrooms and sing my heart out to Goapele $ecret.

I can feel your temperature rise.
Look in my eyes if you looking for love.
Keep what you find.
'Cause I, I got a secret.
Need you to keep it.
Need you to hold it,
Caress it, and squeeze it.
Stay incognito.
From AM to PM.
Keep it on the low.
Can you play in the deep end?
Gotta know if it's worth letting go of my secrets,

CHAPTER 3

Kwame

Gaea being let go puts things into perspective for me. I can no longer sit back and pretend that part of her being fired has nothing to do with me. In fact, that shit has everything to do with me. I'm not even being honest with myself about the shit that happened between Lisette and me. But how can I when I've buried that shit so deep that I'd honestly forgotten all about it.

Back then, I wanted Lisette about as much as I wanted to nurture my friendship with Gaea at the time. Only Lis wasn't checking for me like that, and it fucked with me on a level I can't quite explain. Rejection, I could handle, but fucking me while looking down your nose at me was something entirely different. But I thought with time, I could change her—well, rather when she saw my heart, she would change.

She was the exact opposite of Gaea but everything I needed while in undergrad. The only downfall with her was she wasn't ready to fully commit to me again, fucking me on the low. Lisette didn't push for a commitment with me until she saw that I was for sure a shoo-in for the NFL draft. Then and only then was I good enough to be her man. When that was made clear, she went from being a girl I could wife to, if I'm being completely honest, just some girl I used to fuck.

As I watch her approach my table with a scowl, I feel a bit uneasy. I stand and pull her chair out for her. She sucks her teeth and mutters a half-ass *thank you* under her breath.

"Lisette, I would like to thank you for taking the time out of your busy schedule to meet with me today," I begin as I see her roll her big ass eyes. "I asked you here for a number of reasons but mainly to address the connection between you, Aaron, and Gaea."

"Let me stop you right fucking there. You aren't going to pretend that we"—she waves her hand between the two of us—"don't have a history ourselves."

"Lis—"

"Oh, was I not supposed to say anything about that? Typical Kwame fucking Jacobsen! Despite what you choose to believe, the sun doesn't rise and fall on your ass! So if we are going to get anywhere, let's start with our shit!"

"Our shit?" I ask, clearly confused at the turn of this conversation.

"Yes, our shit! You walked away from me like I wasn't shit! We were rock solid until you decided to do your thing."

"Look now, Lisette, you're making things very personal. I came here to get a better understanding of what exactly is going on so that I won't have to involve anyone else into this mess."

"Flash, you made things very fucking personal when you played with my heart. None of this had anything to do with Aaron and I. Yeah, I may have known him from around the way, but it was you that I was with. I wasn't there as a friend."

"Lisette, none of this makes sense to me. I agree, we fucked around but not to the extent that you are making it out to be. You were fucking Aaron while fucking me; let's not pretend you're innocent in any of this!" I spit out.

"No, Flash, you are definitely not about to make me out to be crazy. That's what we are not gonna do. You and I were a thing. A *real* fucking thing! Stop downplaying shit like it didn't happen. I only fucked around with Aaron so that Gaea could feel everything that I felt. Everything with you was always Gaea! Gaea this! Gaea that! I was so sick and tired of hearing about the bitch! That shit can make the sanest person snap. Never mind the fact that I was at every single one of your games, cooking your meals, fucking you regularly, and washing your dirty ass drawers. So excuse me for not giving a fuck about you, her, yo' daughter, or her fucking job."

"Like, you are making this out to be something it just doesn't have to be. We weren't together, Lis! We were fucking! Man, damn, you were the one that was adamant in letting me know our worlds outside of the bedroom would never coincide. Yes, we fucked around, but at no point did you let me know you changed your mind. Well, you did after I announced my plans to go pro. But that's not relevant. In the beginning, I was truly feeling you. I mean, who wouldn't? You were a beautiful woman, inside and out. I get that you're angry, but at no point should you target innocent people who had no idea we were even fucking around. Especially my daughter, man. So tell me what the fuck you know!"

Lisette takes a moment to look me over before she laughs at me. It's baffling to me that she even feels some kind of way. Sure, I had a crush on Gaea back then, but back then, we were friends. I tried to make Lisette my woman, but she was hell-bent on us not being anything because her parents wouldn't approve, yet she's firing Gaea and approaching me with some age-old bullshit. Bullshit I'm not privy to, because this shit here was already making my head hurt.

"What I know is that you and your wack ass bitch will pay for what you've put me and my man through. This could've all been avoided had you done the right thing and married me."

"Married you? Yo, what the fuck are you even talking about?"

"You will see, Flash! If you would excuse me, I have better things to do rather than sit here shooting the shit with you. Good luck on your search for your brat; I'm sure you'll need it," she spits out as she tosses her purse on her shoulder and storms off out of the restaurant.

All of this shit is baffling to me. Honestly, how's the world this fucked up that my baby's now suffering because of the actions of adults? None of this logically makes any sense. Just as I think my day can't get any worse, I see Maxwell enter the restaurant and makes a beeline directly toward me.

"You done being a little bitch yet? Are you ready to apologize and get back to the money?"

"Max, gone on somewhere with all that shit. I made it clear, as did my lawyers, that I'm not fucking with you in any capacity."

"Man, that shit you pulled was just for show to impress your bi—"

"Let me stop you there before I really have to whoop yo' ass! This doesn't have anything to do with Gaea but everything to do with Kynsley and you trying to play puppeteer with my life! I was more than generous in giving you a severance, so know that I meant what the fuck I said! Coming back here violates the terms of the agreement. Do I need to call my lawyers?"

Maxwell shifts a little on his feet before he clears his throat and makes eye contact with me. "What if I told you I have information on the whereabouts of your daughter?"

I was ready to dismiss his ass before he mentioned Kynsley. I can't let him see how he's piqued my interest, so I play it cool as I lift an eyebrow, signaling him to continue on. He lets out a dry chuckle before he takes another step closer to me and grabs a chair. He uses a hand signal to get the waitress's attention, and after he places an order for a gin and tonic, he continues to silently look me over, I'm guessing to gauge how interested I am in the news he's delivering. My interest is piqued, but I know better than to take anything from Maxwell and run with it. I could be setting myself up to walk into my very own death trap.

"Max, I don't have all day, man! Speak yo' peace or be done with it! Either way, I got shit to do," I demand, clearly agitated. The waitress appears once more, placing his drink in front of him, and then disappears again. He takes a sip of his drink and looks at me.

"You know, son, despite the contempt you feel in your heart for me, know that I do love you. I have a fucked-up way of showing you, but I never wanted you to hurt. By keeping Kynsley and even Gaea away from you, I thought I was helping you to grow. Helping you achieve all the things I couldn't because, well, I just made poor choices. Kwame Langston, I love you, and I've expressed that love the only way I know how," he says before taking another sip from his cup.

I still haven't uttered a word, because what can I really say? That I understand? Because I don't. That I forgive him? That can't be, because I'm not at that point yet. Yes, his opinion is valid because they're his own. They just don't mean anything to me at the moment, so I just sit and wait for him to continue.

"Listen, I know we may never get to a place where we will be like most father and son relationships, but I at least hope that we can get to a place of healing," he says, finishing off his drink "Here is what I know about Kynsley. Some young cat had been asking around the way if there would be someone willing to abduct a little girl. Most of the young niggas said no, all except a Garret. He was bold in his approach. For the most part, I've taken care of him and his family. Go to this address and pick up your baby. She's safe, man. I couldn't be a good man to you, but I need you to be that for her," he says as he pats my back and walks out of the restaurant.

I look down at the paper and jump into action. I call Detective Dawson and give him the address to look into it. Not giving him the chance to brush me off, I let him know that I'll be on my way to check it out myself. I shoot off a mass text to Theodore and Tobias to let them know to drop everything and meet me at that address with Gaea. I pray to God that Maxwell isn't fucking me over or setting me up for an ambush of some sort. All I need at this moment is for Kynsley to be there and to be safe. My life depends on it.

CHAPTER 4

Maxwell

I know I get a bad rap because of the way I treat Kwame, but understand I do it for a reason. I love my son, but I can't stomach to be around him, knowing that his mother pulled some fuck shit. I was a star athlete just as Kwame, but then I met his mother. Karen was so innocent and sweet, but she was also manipulative. I fell head over hills in love with that woman and probably would've married her had she not come to tell me she was pregnant.

I just wasn't ready, and neither was she. We came from nothing and had absolutely nothing but the clothes on our backs, but she wanted to subject a child to that. I'm not rocking with that. After she refused to get rid of the baby, I was angry. My parents made me drop sports in order to get a job. Thank God I was smart enough to get an Academic scholarship. I went to school, worked, and saved my money to support them.

I still did my thing, but I expected more from Karen. She wasn't supposed to stray, especially not while carrying my seed. Nothing broke my heart more than the day we were going to find out the sex of our baby. I walked into the doctor's office after weeks of ignoring her. All that nagging was stressing me out. I already had to give up sports, but hearing her mouth enraged me, so I shut down. When I spotted Karen, she looked so beautiful, and her skin was glowing. It was for that reason that I decided I was done being mad at her and would make an honest woman out of her.

Those thoughts were short-lived when I saw my best friend, James, waltz in and kiss my woman on her forehead. I shat bricks and shut that poor clinic down. Like, of all people, Karen had to go and fuck my best friend. That shit wasn't right, and both of them knew it. I approached them on some chill shit at first, but then James had to open his bitch ass mouth about me fucking other bitches and make Karen cry.

I didn't want her to find out that way, but she did, and I was salty as fuck. I couldn't stop her tears, because I did do the shit, and there wasn't a reason to lie when she would find out the truth anyway. I tried to beat James's face into the receptionists' desk. He knew better, so he had to get that ass beat and would continue to get it beat until I got tired.

When I sat in that jail cell for beating James's ass, I decided then I was done with her ass. She posted my bond and let me know we were having a little boy. She also let me know to stay away from her if I was going to cut a fool every time I saw her. So that's what the fuck I did. Was I wrong? Probably. But it saved us a lot of drama.

The day that Gaea showed up at Kwame's door, I refused to let history repeat itself. I tried to make his life easier. I just didn't count on her to be as stubborn as she was. I just knew she was a groupie trying to come up off my son until I walked into her hospital room and saw a tiny replica of my daughter, Kalyse.

Even after DNA was established, she had to be hidden. After all the hell I gave Kwame, he deserved some peace. I even paid that girl hush money from my own pocket, but nope. She brought her ass back to light, and now my granddaughter is missing. I didn't expect her to stand her ground and check me in front of those people, let alone her job. When I left, I looked into her and found that little bitch was filthy rich. I then regretted my decision to play around in Kwame's life. I just pray the information I give Kwame is valid and that he gets to her before they move her again.

"Man, when are you going to let me go!" Garret howls out.

"Let you go? Nigga, are you crazy?" I spit out.

"I gave you what you needed. I just need to get home to my family. I promise I won't say a word. Just let me go, please!" he pleads.

"Shut the fuck up! You think I give a fuck about your family when you took baby girl away from hers?" I ask as I backhand him.

"I swear I just needed the money," he whimpers out.

"Tell me how much your life is worth!"

"It's worth $25,000."

"Damn, I would've paid you better. Now, who sent you?"

"This old cat. He said if I could bring the mom too, I'd get double. I was going to snatch her that night as well, but I couldn't get close. The only reason I got the little girl is because my girl started flirting with security around the time they were doing costume changes. I grabbed her, figuring $25K is better than nothing. I went back a couple of days later to snatch her, but her man rushed in like Rambo, so I hid in the attic. The shit in baby girl's room was done by some bald-headed chick. They are going to move her again to a different address tonight. That's all I got."

"Thank you for that. I'll see you in hell!" I say before I shoot him right in between the eyes.

I may be a shit father, but I'm prepared to kill everyone who has played a part in my granddaughter's disappearance.

"Clean this shit up. I got moves to make," I call out over my shoulder on my way out the door.

CHAPTER 5

Aaron

*Y*ou never realize how much of a fool you've been in a situation until reality pulls up and sits right on your chest. For years, I've been holding onto a string of hope that Gaea will come back to me, and we'll return to normal. I'll eventually stop cheating and truly be the man that's truly for her. But unfortunately, that time I dreamed of just can't happen; it just isn't in the cards for us.

The day that I pulled up on her in her yard should've put things in perspective for me, but it didn't. Not in the way in which one would think it did, especially not when I have Maxine and Janet in my ear and feeding me poison—poison, which, for years, held me captive and stuck in one era of my life. When I could have been being a better father to my daughter or even following things that I'm passionate about, I was stuck living a dream that's trolling for Janet and Maxine.

After sitting with Kwame those few days I was held captive, something in me woke up. I mean, granted, he shot me, he never once tried to change my mind about the things that I was spewing out at him about Gaea. Never once did he try to change my mind about the poison my mom and Janet was pumping into me. No, Kwame stood stone-faced as I spit out all the shit I was forced to believe. He listened to me without judgement or rebuttal about what I knew in my heart that Gaea felt. No, instead, as he listened to me gripe, I couldn't help but realize that this was the man that was uniquely made for her. Don't get me wrong; I'm still that nigga; I'm just not the nigga for her. I need a fly bitch that'll let me do what I want when I want and how I want, and she just isn't that.

If nothing else, they're truly a match because they're both weird as fuck, and both of their dumbasses shot me. Hell, if that isn't a match, I don't know what is. Nothing made me realize that more than the day I was shot. I know the risk of letting go of Gaea; it means that I may die, but after all the hell that I've caused her, she deserves some happiness. I know that with Kwame, she'll be safe and that her heart will be his number one priority.

This was solidified when he got me the help I needed after I was shot. I was going through a range of emotions, clearly delusional and refusing the help offered, so he had them sedate me. As I drifted in and out of consciousness, I heard Kwame enter the room. I had to make sure I wasn't having a lucid moment before I listened in closely to him praying for me.

"Father God, I come to you as humble as I know how. Forgive me for my sins, Father. I pray that this prayer for peace reaches you in good faith. It is my prayer that you not only heal Aaron physically but that you release him from the bondage holding his life captive. Heal his soul and hold his heart in your grace. When you return it to him brand new, I pray that he's receptive of it. I don't know what you have planned for this young man, but I pray that you humble him enough so that his journey leads him to you. Teach him to walk in your way and to love those close to him with the love of God and not just with eyes of envy or things that they can do for him. It is my prayer that you help him to be a better father to his daughter. I pray that you heal his heart, Lord. And place his heart, his soul and the life you have so graciously given to him back into your hands as his brother. In your name, I do pray. Amen, amen, and amen."

I'm not a soft ass nigga, so I won't allow him to know that that prayer moved me. Not only did it move me, it's also the reason I'm meeting up with my mother and Janet. I can no longer be a pawn in their game of chess, especially not now when I have dirt on them. No matter the outcome of this meeting, I swear I'm done with this chasing Gaea business. I'm tired, and I have the rest of my life to deal with finding the right woman to come into me and Sidney's worlds. There's no use in rushing resentment when the other side of the road offers fulfillment.

"You disappear for an entire week then want a meeting with the both of us? What do you want?" my mother spits out.

"Well, hello to you too, Mother. I'll keep this short, sweet, and to the point. I know that Kynsley isn't my child. You two have been lying to me for the better part of four years. I've been so angry and hyper obsessed with getting Gaea back that any love that was there was lost. I'm not in love with her, and I refuse to ruin Kynsley's life and continue on with this plan! I'm letting you know right here and right now that I'm out!" I declare.

"Aaron, you think because you prepared that little speech and grew some balls during your time away, your job with us is done? Think again! You owe us for keeping your ass afloat. Turn your back on us, and I promise everything you have now will crumble," Janet spits out.

"Janet, I'm OK with that. You also forget that I work. I'm an engineer. I have a degree to fall back on. But what do you two have? Hmmm, let's see. A secret that will destroy both of your marriages and leave y'all trifling asses broke. You see, that manipulative shit may have worked in the past, but know that it doesn't even make me break a sweat now. Strip me blind and rob me of millions. Just know that I am out. My focus going forward will be on my daughter."

"Your daughter, huh? Not if I have anything to do with it. I'll have your ass so tied up in court you'll be spitting up case files! Or better yet, I'll just get rid of her all together!" Maxine whisper-yells then lets out a bloodcurdling laugh.

Before I have time to think about my actions, I have my hands around her throat, squeezing tightly. I play about a lot of things, but when it comes down to Sidney Reneé Williamson, I'm not having it! She had the opportunity to play around with my life, but she won't be able to get to the point where she can hurt Sidney. I'll die trying to save her. The only true innocent people in all of this are the children. All they ever ask for in this world is to be loved. But they've been through hell. Sidney lost her mother to an apparent suicide due to postpartum, and Kynsley is missing!

"You lay one hand on my daughter, and I'll kill you without an ounce of regret. As a matter of fact, stay away from the both of us. If you both know what's best for you, you'd give up the whereabouts for Kynsley because that nigga Flash ain't playing and will blow your brains out through your asshole about his seed! I'm gonna let your ass go, but be warned; I will kill you. Be careful of what you try to do to me. Your secret won't be buried with me!" I say as I release her throat and stand to walk away.

Once I make it to my car, I made the decision to leave town. I won't take any chances. I'm picking my daughter up and leaving everything we had here in this town. I'll rebuild somewhere else. I can't live my life in fear of what will happen to us if we stay. Sidney will understand and thank me for this one day. After packing up a few necessities and picking Sidney up, we head to the airport. I get her settled in and excuse myself to make a quick phone call.

"Hello?" a beautiful, angelic voice calls out, and for a few seconds, I'm taken back to the day we first met.

As I make my way into the foyer, I hear this beautiful voice coming from our family sitting room.

Silly of me to think that you
Could ever really want me too.
How I love you.
You're just a lover out to score.
I know that I should be looking for more.
What could it be in you I see?
What could it be?
Oh... oh... oh... love, oh, love,
Stop making a fool of me.

Like a man caught in the thickest of quicksand or more like drying cement, I'm stuck in one spot, completely lost in a trance. What I may have thought I felt physically for Ana is all but forgotten. This little butterfly with a powerful voice touches my little teenage heart, and it doesn't hurt that she's beautiful. She wears a modest peasant dress paired with gladiator sandals topped off with yellow fingernail polish on her hands and feet and a sunflower headband laying on a cascade of long, flowy curls. I'm so deep in a trance that I don't even realize that she's stopped singing.

"Oh my goodness, I didn't think anyone else was in here. Was I loud? If so, I do apologize. Sometimes, I just get carried away," she stumbles out. Realizing that I'm not saying anything, she continues. "OK... I'm Gaea, but most people call me Butterfly." *She extends her hand out to shake.*

"Nice to meet you, Gaea. I'm Aaron. You have a beautiful voice, unlike that Pitbull of a sister you have there," *I finally force out, grasping her small, delicate hand, and I'm rewarded with a bashful blush.*

"Hello! Is anybody there?" she calls out once more.

"Gaea?"

"Aaron, how the fuck did you get this number? You know what? It doesn't matter. I'm hanging up!" she spits out.

"Butterfly, wait! Don't hang up! I only have a few minutes, so let me say what I need, and I promise to leave you alone for good." I wait a few moments to see if she'll hang up or not. Seeing as she doesn't, I continue. "I want you to know that I never meant to hurt you. I loved you the best way I knew how. I selfishly wanted to keep you near me because your light was the purest form of love I'd ever known. You were rare and so beautiful. Who wouldn't want you as their wife? Over time, I grew to resent you because you never stood up to me. In my eyes, you were becoming my mother—until the day you shot me." I chuckled.

"Aaron, what's the point of this?" she asks, trying to mask the fact that she's crying.

"Butterfly, I'm just wiping our slate clean. You deserve so much more than what I ever gave you. You deserve some peace after all the hell I've put you through. As much as it pains me to say this, that peace you need lays in the heart of Kwame. He's the man God

25

designed just for you. Don't let our mothers get into your head. Those bitches are grimy! I know that your daughter, although beautiful, doesn't belong to me. I wish I knew where she was so that I could bring her back to you. I'm sure wherever she is, those bootleg bitches had something to do with it. Don't trust them. Take care of yourself, beautiful, and know that in my own unique way, I will forever love you."

"Thanks for giving me the closure I needed in this chapter, Aaron. I pray whatever caused you to do this brings you peace. I love you too. Goodbye," she declares as she hangs up the phone, sniffling. No lie, I shed a few tears myself as I hang up the phone. I meant everything I said to her. I need to let her go in order to get to a place of love and healing in my own life. Sidney deserves that. Hell, I deserve that. As I collect my daughter to board that plane, I toss that phone and never look back.

"You ready to explore the world, kid?"

"Yes, Daddy! Let's go!"

CHAPTER 6

Gaea

I've been lying around in my own misery for a few days now. I honestly see no point in getting out of the bed. Since I couldn't stomach looking at him, I had subjected myself to sleeping in one of the guest rooms. It was best before I continued to pump out poison between us. I have no leads on finding Kynsley, Kwame's sick of my shit, and Lisette pulled a whole bitch move and fired me. I still don't know how that happened, but shit it did, and there's nothing I can do to change it. So yeah, I've been sitting in this bed, drowning. I can't even rely on Ana, because she told me until I stopped being selfish, I need not call her. So much for that damn sisterly love. I'm truly on my own.

"Gaea, get yo' ass up out of that bed so we can talk. There is no use in laying in that bed when Kynsley is still missing. Make better use of your time!" Tobias calls out, interrupting my peace.

"Look, Tobias, I'm not with your shit today. I'm well aware of my daughter being missing. But what the fuck am I supposed to do? Am I to camp out at Ana's studio? Am I to go fuck Aaron to get clues? Since everyone knows so fucking much about what I'm supposed to be doing, tell me why in the fuck haven't y'all found her yet! Huh?" I spit out.

"Aight, I thought I wouldn't have to resort to this, but you two blind muthafuckas would drive Jesus to drink! Hear me and hear me clearly when I say this is what the fuck you are gonna do. Get the fuck up and get yo' funky ass in the shower. You have fifteen minutes to get dressed and meet me at my truck. We got shit to do, and coddling yo' ass ain't gonna get it done!" he spits out and slams the guest bedroom door.

Sensing he's serious, I quickly get up and handle my hygiene. I throw on my favorite Omondi "Niggas" pullover paired with Nike compression shorts and my Air Max 270. I give myself a onceover and head down the stairs, throwing my hair into a quick messy ponytail. As I'm coming down the stairs, I hear, "Nah, Gaea, go put on some fucking clothes! Ain't nobody trying to hear Kwame's mouth today!"

"First off, he's not my man, and he's for damn sure not my daddy! He is Kynsley's, so I'll wear what I damn well please," I spit out.

"Have it your way! Let him talk that shit when I'm not around," he says while looking at his phone "Oh shit! You really don't have a choice but to wear that shit now. Hurry up and get yo' ass in the car."

I roll my eyes because I've had enough of him bossing me around. Disregarding everything he's said and the clear urgency in his voice, I walk over to the refrigerator and grabbed a Greek yogurt and a bottle of Bai Malawi Mango. I'm hungry, and if I have to listen to his ass anymore, I know I need to put something on my stomach. Before I even have the chance to open my yogurt, Tobias has thrown me over his shoulder and shoved me into his truck. If he were any other person, I would have cursed his ass all the way out, but being that my number of friends is dwindling, I instead choose to give him a nasty side-eye while mumbling under my breath.

"You can buck yo' eyes until them shits fall out; quite frankly, I don't give a fuck. My niece is far too important to let you, Kwame, and all the bullshit y'all bring to the table silence me. I did that before, and look where it's gotten us. I don't need yo' ass to respond!" He sneers before he continues. "Flash texted me a little bit ago and told

28

me to bring you to an address. Before you start jaw jacking, just listen. They have strong suspicion to believe that Kynsley is inside. I'm not wanting you to get your hopes up, but I instead want you to prepare yourself for whatever is behind those doors."

"Wait... what?"

"You heard me right. We think we have a lead on where Kynsley is."

I take a moment to catch my breath. This just doesn't seem real. We've been searching for weeks with no leads, and now my daughter is within my reach. Well, hopefully. I don't want to get my hopes up only to be let down, so I pray.

"Father, I know that you are my strength when I am weak. Your peace and your love surpass all understanding. You are my voice when I can't speak and my encouragement when my world is gray. I am putting Kynsley's life in your hands. Please lead me safely through. Guide not only my body but also my mind and heart to navigate the way. My trust is fully in you. Amen."

Tobias looks over at me and mumbles, "Amen," as he pulls us into a quiet subdivision. You know, the typical house with a white picket fence, two-car garage, and two point five kids neighborhoods. By glance, nothing seems strange, but the feeling in the pit of my stomach is telling me something's wrong. I run over multiple different scenarios in my head on how this can play out. In my heart of hearts, I know that my baby's alive. God wouldn't take her from me this soon. I just know that, but what I can't say for certain is that she'll come out of this unharmed and with the same youthful innocence that makes her uniquely mine. Kynsley is the right in the world that I need.

As we pull up to a cottage-style home, I see Kwame and immediately jump out of the moving car and run straight to him, firing off questions a mile a minute.

"Why didn't you call and tell me, Kwame? Stop being so fucking childish by not communicating with me!" I spit out.

"Look, Gaea, now is not the time for that bullshit! I did it because I didn't want you to hurt your fucking self by trying to get over here. I knew Tobias was swinging by to talk to you, so I told him to bring you here to me. You're here now, so stop complaining! Damn! I can't win for losing with yo' ass!"

"You still should've been the one to tell me, and I'm firm on that," I say, placing my hands on my hips, drawing his eyes to my outfit.

"Man, gone on with all of that noise. You here now, so shut up about it. What you need to worry about is going to get some fucking pants out of my trunk," he spits out, clearly dismissing my entire argument. Feeling frustrated, I storm off to approach Detective Dawson. I want to see if I can get more information that I'm not getting from Kwame but not before I hear him say, "Aight, bet."

I badger Detective Dawson for a good forty-five minutes before his partner finally tells me they're waiting for a judge to sign off on a search warrant. Feeling defeated for wasting so much of my time, I make my way back over to Kwame, Tobias, and now my father. It amazes me how close the two have become in such a short span of time. If I'm not mistaken, I swear they spend more time on the phone than I do, and he's my dad.

The entire time my dad and Kwame talk, I try my best not to give him an ounce of attention; instead I focus on the officer and Tobias. Just as I'm about to bulldoze into their conversation, I feel Kwame's breath tickling the back of my neck as he places his arm around my waste.

"Gypsy, I'm not gonna tell you again to put on some fucking pants. Either you're going to walk over there on your own, or I'm going to drag yo' ass over there my damn self, embarrassing us both, yo' daddy be damned. You got five seconds to decide," he growls.

"You're not my man, Kwame!" I spit out. What the fuck did I say that for? All of a sudden, I'm looking at the ground and being carried to his car. He puts me down and throws a pair of pants at me. From the look on his face, I clearly know I've fucked up worse than I had when he told me about Aaron. But what he doesn't get is that I don't give a fuck about Aaron. It's him ruining his life over Aaron that stresses me out.

That gutted me. Aaron was a poster child and could get away with anything he damn welled pleased. We grew up with these people. Hell, if I'm being frank about it, our parents run these circles. We're the Crème De La Crème. Aaron can get off easily for doing whatever he wants to him. The simple fact of the matter is that Kwame can't. He came from nothing, so I'm not about to let him ruin it over a past that Aaron and I share.

Sure, he has money now, but it isn't old money like ours, so I don't expect him to understand why I reacted the way that I did. His protection is key. Hell, I love him, but I can't continue to be the reason that the both of us keep taking losses. He can't be my man until all of this shit we're going through is put to rest permanently. As it stands now, we don't have our daughter, Aaron's still crazy, and I don't even have a damn job. So, no, Kwame isn't my man. He just can't be.

"You're abso-fucking-lutely right, Gaea. You've made it clear in your fucked-up way in treating me that I'm not your man. Quite frankly, I'm done trying to be. There are hundreds of women vying for a single moment of my time, and here you have it and never gave a fuck about it! Hear me and hear me good. I'm good on you!" he spits out.

"But Kwame—" I start to say.

"Nah, ain't no fucking buts. Kill that. As the mother of my child, I expect more—no, I fucking require more out of you than to dress in the manner in which you have. That shit you have on should be worn in the house only. Have more respect for not only yourself but for our daughter than to be out showing the world what little ass you do have. Put the fucking pants on, and don't say shit else to me unless it concerns our daughter," he growls before he walks off.

Before I have the opportunity to pick my face up off the ground and respond to him, a loud boom brings me to my knees. Through my tears, I begin hoping and praying that my last prayer isn't in vain. All around me, all I hear is yelling. Opening my eyes, I see everything move in slow motion. Kwame's yelling out instructions for his camp to search the premises as he sprints into the house with Tobias and my father on his heels.

"Somebody get an EMT in here, now!" I hear Tobias yell back out of the open door. "What the fuck are y'all waiting on! Move mutha-fuckas, move!"

All around me, people spring into action while my feet stay cemented to the ground. I can't force myself to move because of the fear of the unknown. It seems like a lifetime has passed before I see Kwame rush out with our baby clinging to his soot-covered body. All of the first responders begin to rush them.

"Everybody back the hell up! Where were y'all at when I was running into that damn house? Don't fucking touch us! Gaea, get in the goddamn car!" Kwame bellows out, handing me our daughter.

"Kwame, she needs to be seen! Look at her!" I plead with him.

"She will, just not here. You act like you don't see all these damn cameras," he says before he pulls out of the subdivision.

CHAPTER 7

Kwame

*N*ow that the adrenaline has worn off, I'm paying for what I've done. My body is hurting all over, but I'll do it again if that means I'll save Kynsley. My heart shattered when I burst into their world, and I saw my baby girl all dirty and bloody. I can't believe that actions of my and Gaea's past is the reason my baby girl is in the situation at all. I guess Maxwell was good for something. I'll thank him for his help one day, but today just isn't it. For now, I need to get to the bottom of who did this and why.

In my head, I know that Aaron isn't here, but I know that something he has done or was told is the reason my baby is here in this hospital. Janet not being able to be reached is another reason I'm on edge, but for now, I need to make sure that everything is OK with Kynsley and that I have her and her mother safe. But let the record state that I'll be checking the fuck out of Janet, Theodore be damned. Her absence has to mean something. At first, I thought everything was all good, and she was changing her ways for the sake of her children. But nah, this bitch is moving shady as hell. I don't know if Theodore has noticed or if he even cares anymore, but I'm not going to tolerate that shit in any capacity.

"Mr. and Mrs. Jacobsen, I need you all to follow me. The doctor will see you now," the nurse calls out.

"So we meet again but this time with a different Jacobsen child. Your daughter is very lucky to be alive. Although malnourished, she is blessed to come out with only a few broken bones. There were no signs of sexual assault, but at this point, we aren't ruling it out. Kynsley is a very strong little girl, but mentally, she will need to see a therapist. I'm concerned there will be some post-traumatic stress as a result of being held captive for so long. For now, we're keeping her sedated so that she's not in a lot of pain, and we're giving her body time to heal. It's imperative that we use kid gloves with her and let her talk about her experience on her own time. As anxious as we are to know about her experience, we do not want to hinder her healing in any way. I'm going to give you a card of a friend of mine who special-izes in child psychology. You will need it. But for now, we are going to move her to a wing where it is not easily accessible due to your celebrity."

"Thank you, Dr. Milo. I appreciate all of your efforts in taking care of my daughter."

"It's my duty. But I also need to check you out, Mr. Jacobsen."

"I'm fine. Just focus on Kynsley. I want you to focus on making sure that everything is OK with her."

"Have it your way, but do not, under any circumstances, leave this hospital without checking with me," he says as he goes to exit the room.

Gaea's standing at our daughter's bedside, silently weeping. I know that it's taking a lot out of her, and I know that she's hurting, but her actions in regard to me and my heart were inexcusable. Everything I said to her, I meant it. I know in my heart, I'm right, but I want to bend to make it so we can get back to the love we shared. I wish I could take all of the pain, all the betrayal, all the drama, but I can't. There's no way I can make her see that her heart is safe with me, and in all seriousness, I'll no longer force it. She has to see it for herself. But until then, I'm going to do me.

"Gaea, let's go into the hallway and chat for a second."

"Kwame, I'm not leaving my baby's side. Whatever it is you think you need to say, you're going to have to say it right here," she says, clearly agitated.

"You're all about energy and it being transferred, so in order for her to heal positively, we need to clear the air."

"Fine! Let me call Jenn to come in and watch her."

After a few moments, Jenn steps into the room.

"We should only be gone for at most fifteen minutes," Gaea announces.

"Mmhmmm. Gyal don't be a jackass. Mi kno a gud man wen mi si one. Just don't let him tek yuh fi idiot," Jenn says in Patois.

"Yuh gyal inna gud hands," I say while winking.

"You speak the language?" she asks, sounding shocked.

"Not fluently. But yes, I do a little bit," I reply with a wink.

"Cool tings," Jenn says.

We enter the hallway, and immediately she starts jaw jacking. I hate when she does that shit. Like she's so adamant on being the masculine presence in this relationship that she's always barking down my neck. She's so focused on me potentially fucking up that she's unintentionally or intentionally never giving me the opportunity to lead as the masculine presence in her life. I can't rock with that, not even for a moment.

"Yo, kill that noise. I don't have the energy to hear that shit tonight! From this moment moving forward, I need to know all there is to know about you and Kynsley. All that keeping secrets shit is dead. If I find out you're lying to me, you'll live to regret that shit. Understand, I don't give a fuck about you saying I'm not your man. You mine whether you like it or not, but I won't press your ass over it. Do you, but know although you are mine, I won't wait around on your ass. My main concern is keeping you and Kynsley safe. You will have security detail 24/7, and I'm firm on that. We may have Kynsley back, but I'm almost certain this roller coaster isn't over," I tell her.

"OK, fine! But are you going to date?" she asks.

"Since I'm not your man, you don't get to ask me shit like that," I say while walking off from her. She can play those mind games with her damn self; I'm not up for it. To make sure she's to stay in my home, her father and I put her house on the market. If all else fails, I'll move into my downtown condo to give her the space she needs. But for now, I'm not going to worry about that. Hell, I need to take Dr. Milo up in his offer to be seen and to get ready for the press release of us locating Kynsley.

CHAPTER 8

Maxwell

Something just isn't sitting right with me. Kwame reached out to let me know that Kynsley was safe. He thanked me and wanted me to meet her so that she could meet the man who saved her life. I'm in this hospital, but I feel uneasy, especially since this bitch Rebekah I used to dick down keeps staring at me. I knew her type when I fucked her; the husband is always working, so I need me some outside dick to tighten me up until he gives me some attention. Yeah, she's the typical scorned ass housewife with nothing to do but complain and spend her husband's money on bullshit. Her pussy is mediocre at best, so I can see why her husband works the way he does.

"Yes, Maxine, they found her. I don't have any more information. Theodore said it wasn't important; I just needed to be a mother. So here I am, waiting to do the motherly thing," Rebekah says.

"Get your ass off that phone. Maxine isn't immediate family, and last I checked, she didn't give a fuck about our daughters. Hang that phone up, Janet," a large man, I'm assuming was her husband, Theodore, growled out.

"Girl, I got to go. Daddy has spoken," she says, letting out a nervous giggle.

Janet? Who the fuck is Janet? And why is she here? Before I can get my thoughts together, Kwame and Gaea are coming out the door to greet me. Nothing prepares me for the moment my son embraces me.

"Dad... Max... Hell, I don't know what to call you," he says, letting out a nervous chuckle "All I can really say is thank you. I don't know what you did to get that information, but I'm thankful you found it in your heart to do it. I could never repay you for the amount of joy you've restored in my life. I would like for this to be the stepping stone in us actually developing a relationship."

"Son, I meant what I said at that table. I may be a shit father, but I love you. She is my flower as a result of my seed reproducing and making me an old man!" I say, patting his back laughing to keep the tears I had from falling. Before I can end the hug with my boy, I feel a tap on my arm.

"I know we may never see eye to eye, and I'm completely OK with that. I just want you to know that I genuinely appreciate what you have done for Kwame and I. Since you are the reason she is back, we would like to properly introduce you to her," she says while taking a step forward to shake my hand.

"Gaea, it would be my pleasure to meet your little princess," I say while pushing her hand aside and hugging her and placing a kiss on her frontal lobe.

"Great. Give us a moment to get her together, and I will bring you all back," she says while grabbing at Kwame's hand with Theodore on their heels.

As soon as they disappear in the back, Rebekah... Janet... whoever the fuck she is, makes her way over to me.

"What the fuck are you doing here, Max? Are you stalking me?" She sneers.

"Bitch, are you looney? Did you not just see me talking to my son and your daughter? Your pussy was trash, ma. Definitely not worth stalking, so take your loose-neck ass on somewhere," I say, dismissing her.

"You weren't saying that while you were fucking me. How much to make you disappear? I'm not trying to have any more issues with my family and friends. You look like trouble! Trouble that I don't fucking need!"

"As much as you'd like to think that the offer is tempting, it's not. My main goal is to make sure Kynsley is safe. Since you all up in my shit, let me call some people to check you out," I say. As soon as I mention looking into her, this bitch gets all jittery. Even if she doesn't physically lay her hands on my grandbaby, I know now that she played a hand in the shit. When I get done at this hospital, my first plan of action is to look into her and her friends.

I wait for approximately forty-five minutes before I'm allowed to go back into the room. I can admit that I'm calm when Kwame calls and even when Janet was jaw-jacking, but seeing baby girl with her arm in a sling and all bruised tossed all that shit out the window. If Garrett weren't already dead, I would put more than one bullet in his ass.

"Bumblebee, I need you to wake up for a minute. There is someone I'd like for you to meet."

"Mommy, I want Daddy," her little voice croaks out.

"I'm right here, Princess. I would like for you to meet my father, Maxwell."

"Hello there, sweetheart. I know you're tired, so I won't stay long."

"Hi, Father Maxwell. I Kynsley. I not tired; I just scared. Are you going to bring that mean old man back to hurt me? He shakes me hard when I cry for Mommy and Daddy," she says, looking around skittishly while cradling her arm.

"No, baby, I would never bring anyone around to harm you, but I will find that sapsucker who did it and make him pay for what he's done to you."

"So you are nice, Father Maxwell?"

"Just call me Pop Pop, princess. I wasn't nice before, but I will be nice to you."

"I would love you forever if you tell Mommy and Daddy to get some ice cream," she says, getting out of the bed to come over and hug me.

"How about I let you rest and take your daddy with me to go get the ice cream?" I ask her.

"That's fine, but you two come right back," she says while limping back over to her mother. Seeing her limp further breaks my heart. This is a child that's been dragged into adults' bullshit. I can't bring myself to understand it. Even with all the bad shit I've done with Kwame, I never thought once that I should hurt his kid, so these muthafuckas had to pay.

As Kwame and I head to the elevator, the little bald-headed gray-eyed bitch that was always making her way around him in college is walking briskly away from Janet's sneaky ass. It's then that I realize I'm going to have to kill her ass. One thing about it; I've never trusted a snake, and her ass is moving shifty as hell.

"Flash, I'm telling you this so that you can hold your girls up when the shit hits the fan, but, um, I'm going to kill whoever is responsible for harming Kynsley. Now, I don't need you to say anything. Just follow out to get baby girl her ice cream," I say. He nods his head and continues with his conversation about securing his compound. He may not have taken heed to my warning, but the darkness of destruction is upon us.

A few weeks later...

I've been following Janet's trifling ass for a few days now, and this bitch moves just like I thought—shady as fuck. It's clear she doesn't give a flying fuck about that Theodore nigga she's married to. The evidence is in her standing appointment at the Hyatt she's been visiting every day at noon for the last couple of weeks. I never see her go in with anyone, but I know her ass isn't having lunch. I sat in the restaurant to see for myself; I waited for hours one day just to see what I would find.

The only thing I've come up with is her coming out with a light-skinned woman with some horrible ass weave. But I know there has to be more to that story. That woman with the weave is throwing me off for a number of reasons. Reason one, they were to close for my liking and the most important reason was I just don't trust a woman's judgement that walks around with trash ass weave. If you don't care about your weave, you don't care about your life.

I'll never understand how women can spend all this money on their hair for it to come out looking like shit, especially women with money. They know better. They make too much money to be walking around looking ugly with that tired ass weave. That'll drop a woman that's a ten to a two in my book. That shit literally grinds my gears, but whatever.

Pushing those thoughts aside, I hurry along to the elevator. I pay off the front desk clerk as well as the housekeeper to give me the information and the keys that I need to handle business. I stand outside and wait a few minutes until I feel they're settled and comfortable before I silently enter the room.

"Oh shit, baby... Right there... Don't stop... Ahhh," I heard Janet moan out. If I didn't know that this bitch's pussy was trash, it would probably make my dick hard. As I walk further into the room, I don't know what I expected to see, but it certainly wasn't Janet spread eagle with that bad-weave-wearing bitch's face pushed deep within her pussy walls. I stand and watch them for a moment more. These hoes are freaks. I would have never, for one moment, taken her for being lesbian, but hey. It gives a better explanation to her not fully engaging in sex with me.

"Shit, Maxine, I'm about to cum!" she screamed out.

"You might want to hold that nut, you sick bitch!" I chuckled. You would think these duck ass broads had been shot by the way they fall out of the bed and scatter away from each other. They do all of that but forget to cover their bodies up.

"How the fuck did you know where to find me? You really couldn't get enough of this pussy, huh?"

"Now, bitch, you just running out. I don't know how many times I have to tell yo' ass that shit was mediocre at best, and I'm being generous with the compliments here," I say, trying not to look as disgusted at her having the gall to keep disrespecting me like that.

"Fuck all of that! How the fuck did you get in here?" Maxine snarled out.

"Honestly, that shit doesn't matter. I'm in here now. So the better question is, why the fuck did you loose pussy hoes snatch Kynsley? I mean, I don't get that shit, especially coming from you, Janet. That's your granddaughter!"

"Let's not pretend that you're Granddaddy of the year here, Maxwell. You don't give a fuck about that little girl. You are just trying to get back in the good graces of Flash!" Janet says in a huff.

"Man, y'all need to put some drawers on or something. I'm not about to keep having this conversation with y'all ran-through ass pussies hanging out and shit! Like, for real, have y'all thought about pussy rejuvenation? Tighten that shit up," I say while walking across the room to collect the cameras that I had set up in the room earlier. You have to cover your tracks with these two. They'll have you out there looking a fool if you aren't careful.

"Fuck you, Maxwell!" Janet yells as she throws her clothes on.

"So again, I ask you, why would you do this?"

"We didn't take Kynsley, if that's what you're thinking. That couldn't be further from the truth, but it worked in our favor. With Kynsley out of the way, that opened the door for Gaea and Aaron to get together so that we could begin our efforts to truly be together!" Maxine declares.

"So y'all can be together? Do you know how crazy you sound? Y'all bitches can be together without making these kids' lives hell."

"Aaron and Gaea's marriage would bring in millions of dollars. We would be financially set for life and able to leave our limp-dick husbands alone and finally divorce them," Maxine says matter-of-factly.

"I don't know about your husband, but ain't nothing limp about Theodore's dick!" Janet smirks out while licking her lips.

"Bitch, you still fucking him?"

"Duh, bitch, every chance I get," Janet says with a shrug.

"Maxine, you do know those kids have to actually like each other? You aren't God. You hoes can't force shit that ain't supposed to be!

Y'all can't be this stupid. You couldn't have thought this shit through," I say, looking at both of their confused asses.

"I may not be God, but I can make shit happen like only God can!" Maxine shouts.

"Now I for real know yo' ass is crazy. Obviously, that decrepit ass pussy has you a few marbles short of being the next Judas, but keep that blasphemous shit to yourself. If you can make shit happen, how come you can't stop this hoe from fucking you, Theodore, and your husband all within the same week?" I ask as I begin to collect the things I need.

"You're fucking who, bitch?" Maxine asks as she jumps across the bed to beat the fuck out of Janet. Seeing as my work is done with these two hags, I go and tip my two little helpers and go on with the rest of my day. I can't wait to drop this shit off to their husbands.

CHAPTER 9

Gaea

*E*ach day, I feel so blessed to be looking at you
    'Cause when you open your eyes, I feel alive.
My heart beats so damn quick when you say my name.
When I'm holding you tight, I'm so alive.
Now let's live it up.

"Mommy, I like it when you sing that song for me."

"Bumblebee, Mommy likes singing them to you. Now let's get you dressed so we can get our day started."

It has been a couple of weeks since my baby was released from the hospital, but we still want to play things safe. Kwame and I decided it'll be best if we all stay under one roof. So although we aren't speaking, we try our best to put on the brave front in front of our daughter. For the most part, she seems to enjoy having us both in close proximity, so for now, I'll continue to do what I need to do to make our daughter happy.

As I make my way to the kitchen, I hear laughter. Kwame didn't say anything about having guests, so it all comes as a surprise. Seeing a stunned Ana, I turn to quickly make an exit.

"I'm sorry. I didn't mean to interrupt. I was just coming down to get Kynsley something to drink after taking her medicine," I say, trying to make a quick exit.

"Gaea, please don't leave," I heard Ana plea.

"I don't have it in me to argue, especially with Kynsley nearby, so I'm going to get her juice and go."

"Gaea, sit yo' ass down. Y'all are going to handle this shit today! Kay, goes upstairs and see about your niece. I'll let you know when Kion is ready to take y'all to the art gallery," Kwame's voice booms with him never placing his eyes on me.

"OK. Sorry, Gaea. The boss has spoken." Kalyse giggles. We wait a bit until we hear the door to Kynsley's bedroom door close.

"Ana, say what you need to say. No need in carrying this shit on when Gaea and Kwame are now living together. Fix this shit!" Tobias demands.

"Butterfly, I know some of the things I said were harsh. But understand, they were coming from a loving place. I get so frustrated when you never admit your own faults, but you're so quick to look down your nose at others for theirs," Ana says.

"That's not what I was doing, and you know that!" I argue.

"But it is! You didn't give him a chance. You looked down your nose at him as if he were Aaron or even Janet. Hell, you did the same with Maxwell, and look how wrong you were. The same thing you're trying to shield Kynsley from is the very thing you're instilling in her," Ana berates.

"I've never, not even once, looked down my nose at *anyone*. So don't you sit there with that smug ass look on your face and tell me I did. Yes, I was wrong about Maxwell, but in my heart of hearts, I still don't think it is Aaron. Just because I don't think he's capable of harming Kynsley doesn't mean that I love him! In fact, it's quite the opposite! He was a huge part of my life for so long, so I'm pretty sure I know his heart. Outside of his cheating, he is a pretty decent individual. He wouldn't harm a child. But I won't get the chance to ask him anything, being as this bozo killed him!" I yell out, causing Kwame to choke on my damn Bai water.

45

"Whoa, wait a fucking minute here! I didn't kill anyone! I don't know where the fuck you got that information from, but stop spreading that damn lie. Yeah, I shot his ass, but he isn't dead!" he yells, invading my space.

"Right, you shot him, so where the fuck is he? Maxine called me, talking about going to the police because Aaron is missing, and I was the last person he called!" I say, revealing too much. I can't possibly tell him that Aaron had called and gave me the closure I so desperately need to be with him. My pride won't allow it, not when he's keeping his word about not checking for me in any capacity.

Our home, from the outside looking in, is perfect. Perfect in the fact that PR never lets anything remotely bad about either of us get out. I just look like the perfect housewife without being an actual wife. Even though he told me not to worry about what he does, I've seen the lipstick stains on his shirt when he comes home and smells like cheap ass Bath & Body Works perfume. I'm not judging the hoe, but I'm judging his ass. He can do much better than the bitch he's fucking with, I'm sure of it.

"Gaea, why the fuck are you even talking to that bitch?" Ana yells, breaking me from my thoughts.

"So we are still keeping shit from each other, Gypsy? I know I made myself clear when I told yo' ass to stop hiding shit from me!" Kwame crosses the room and whispers in my ear. To make matters worse, he licks my ear then bites down on it. I hate when he takes control, and my body gives in to submission. Granted, we haven't touched each other since the day I kicked that bathroom door in. But now my body's heating up, so I know I need to move.

"Watch out now, Kwame! You play too much. Ain't nobody hiding nothing from you," I say, trying to move past him, but he grips me by my waist and rubs his semi-erect penis across my ass. You know what my dumb ass has the audacity to do? My super horny ass moans. The shit is so loud and awkward that Tobias chokes on his bacon, and Ana lets out a low whistle. I don't know why they're minding my business when they've yet to be upfront with their own.

"Who's playing, Gypsy?" he asks as he runs his fingers along the hem of my dress. "You so nasty, baby. You don't have on any panties."

"Kwame, move now!" I say, brushing past him. "Ana, babe, I love you. Although I wish we could have the same outlook on things, we don't, but we can agree to disagree and get right back to loving one another." I can't even focus on whatever the hell Ana's saying, because Kwame is again behind me, rubbing my ass with his dick. I go to move again, but he has me trapped with both hands on the countertop. He bites down on my neck then kisses it to take the sting out of it. His stupid ass is rubbing his dick all over my ass, making me wet.

"If you moan, I'm going to toss you over my shoulders and take you upstairs and fuck the shit out of you. You have been warned," he whispers in my ear.

"Y'all so fucking nasty! Get out of here with all of that," Tobias chokes out while Ana gives me the *bitch, you better hop on that* look.

"Stop, Kwame, you play too much." I moan again

"Whelp, y'all, it's been real. I warned her ass," he says while tossing me over his shoulder and carrying me up the stairs.

As soon as we make it to the master bedroom, he pulls my dress over my head and kisses me with so much passion I swear he takes my soul. In his kiss, I feel everything he no longer has the courage to tell me, everything he hoped we could be, everything he told me was no longer available to me. Why has it taken me so long to realize the depth of his love? How long have I been blinded by the hurt of lovers' past that I so stubbornly pushed him away?

As good as he's making me feel, it just feels so wrong. Wrong because, in his words, we won't be anything more than co-parents, and I can't put my heart through that. I just can't allow that no matter what.

"Gypsy, I meant what I said when I said you were mine. I meant it down to every single syllable. This, as well as your heart, belongs to me and me only. I'm the only nigga that better have a key to your heart and the only one to get this thang wet," he says as he pins me against the wall and starts strumming my clit and prepping my pussy for entry. It's like my body wakes up for him when he's talking shit. I can go from Sahara Desert dry to full-on tsunami in a matter of seconds.

"Kwame, baby, you said..." I moan out, enjoying the attention he's paying to my neck and clit. The more he strums, the harder he sucks on my neck. I'm not a fool; I know his ass is doing this to purposely mark what he deems his territory.

"Fuck what I said, Gypsy. You're mine. I don't know why you keep holding yourself back from me. You are safe with me. I got you, baby. I just want to love you and to get that same love in return," he whispers in my ear as he enters my love canal slowly, giving me inch after delicious inch.

"Shit, Kwame, you feel so fucking good," I moan out as he captures my mouth.

"Tell me you want it too, baby," he says while increasing speed. I can't find or form the words to speak to him to let him know that I want it just as bad as he does. As he digs deeper and deeper into my body, it's like a dam breaks, and instead of rejoicing in this orgasm, I pick my heart up off the floor. Kwame releases his seeds in me and lies with me in his arms, silently contemplating his next words. He sits up on the floor and kisses my forehead before he says, "I love you, Gaea Lee. But I refuse to break my own heart while chasing after yours." When he disappears into the bathroom, I quickly dress and head down the stairs and out of the house, and I collapse into Anais's arms, letting out a bloodcurdling cry.

"I lost him, Ana! I really fucking lost him, and I only have myself to blame!" I scream.

That night was the hardest thing for me. I tossed and turned all night; my nerves had me constantly with my head in the toilet, and for the life of me, I can't shake this headache no matter what I do. I ease out of bed and do the best thing possible for me; I begin to write.

Drifting.
Floating.
Anxiety rising.
Damn, I wish these feelings would fade.
How long have I been foolish?

How often had I been blind?
How long have I suppressed the pain?
Empty.
Why do I feel so drained?
Numb.
Incomplete.
Drowning.
Suffocating.
I need to feel something other than rage.
I need to breathe freely.
I long for my heart to feel comfort.
I'm praying for a clean heart and wild and free spirit.
Reprieve.
What did I do to deserve this?
Loyalty has placed me in a permanent cell.
Anger has become my blanket.
Resentment has become my bed.
I'm carrying this burden on my shoulders.
Lord, please help me to lighten my load.
Can someone love me in this current state?
All broken and bruised?
Can someone restore the light that was taken from me?
Does my frailness frighten you?
Does this...
Me...
Pain...
Run you away?
Can you hear my uncertainty?
Can you smell my fear?
I promise it's not on purpose; it's just my past kinda haunts me.
Visions of him, visions of her, visions of them.
Visions of him giving her everything I thought was reserved and belonging to me.
Can you bring nourishment to my soul?
Do you care enough to smooth out my edges?

The dark, the ugly, and rough spots?
Come love the pain away.
Come forth and make me whole.
Speak to the woman in me and help me to grow.
Caress my heart.
Penetrate my soul.
Speak to my spirit.
Help me to draw my strength from you.
Let me love you from my broken space; I promise you won't regret it.
We can heal my broken heart and get to the best version of me.
Can you see with your heart the beauty of loving me?
My strength, I'm convinced, is God's sacred gift.
Come sail away with me.
The promise of us is sweet.
Casting away all fears and reservations.
Just you and I.
Drifting.
Floating.
Growing in love.

I write until sleep eventually finds me. I find strength behind my pen, so I make the decision then and there that regardless of whatever Kwame and I were going through and the fact the status of our relationship was on chill, I knew I needed to take this opportunity of not working and pour life and love into our daughter's healing. There's no use in nursing my wounds and feelings when Kynsley's still healing from hers. What I feel or don't feel is taking a backseat, starting today.

CHAPTER 10

Kwame

I fucked her. I can't believe I broke my promise to myself to leave her ass alone. Like I've said countless times before, I know Gypsy is it for me, but I'm not about to chase her and beg her ass to be with me. That shit is exhausting. But I set myself up for this insane amount of torture when I thought we could live together and co-parent with the complete understanding that there would be nothing remotely romantic happening. I played myself with that backward ass thought.

As it already stands, I'm torturing myself by watching her play around with Kynsley in those tight ass Nike compression shorts she likes to wear. What makes matters worse is that she's gained a little weight, so that ass is sitting right in those shorts, and don't get me started on the way her breasts are sitting nice as fuck in her shirt. Gaea has me beating my dick nightly. I was doing good, steering clear of her, until she decided she was going to lie to me about her phone call with Maxine. She gave herself away before I even processed the fact that she was lying.

The killing part was that she failed to mention Aaron, but I knew that they had spoken. I heard her when she stepped out on the balcony to take his call. It was one of those rare instances where Kynsley was having trouble sleeping, so we would all camp out in her king-size bed. I assume she thought I was asleep, but I heard her ass say that she loved him too.

Any other man would've been upset, but not me. I'm never one to be insecure by any means, so I'm certain that he was giving her the closure she so desperately needed. Only I'm not waiting around for her to figure shit out. I've done all I can do to get her to see that we need each other, and she continues to treat me horribly. You can't keep doing what you want to me, thinking I'll always be around.

That's the textbook definition to insanity if you ask me, which is why I began to see Melody. I can't keep putting myself in situations where I'm destined to fail. Mel provides a relief for me, and everything's easy. I'm able to be masculine and let her pour all of the femininity she has in her possession into my soul. She's a beautifully, feisty woman who knows what she wants and doesn't have a problem letting you know.

She stands at about five feet seven and holds a great resemblance to actress Regina Hall. She's well educated and knows her way around a camera. In fact, I met her when I was leaving Tobias' office. He told me to stay away from her until I dealt with my feelings—or lack thereof—for my situation with Gaea. He doesn't realize that I'm tired of playing this rollercoaster game with her. I'm going to get my happiness even if it isn't with her.

Melody provides that for me. She doesn't push for a commitment from me. She knows we're just having fun. Even with all of that, I still wasn't honest with her about why we could never go to my home. It's not her business where I lay my head, but the real truth of the matter is I just don't want to hurt Gaea. It pulled at my heartstrings to see her run out of the house and collapse into Anais's arms, but she brought that on herself. Still, it doesn't stop me from feeling guilty about seeing Melody.

It has been a few weeks since Melody and I started connecting. There isn't a time that I have a free moment that we aren't either together or on the phone. No matter how hard I try to fight it, the feelings are forever constant and growing. But I can't bring myself to even acknowledge them or commit to her and truly make her mine. Not when I know that Gaea's where my heart is. I'm confusing the hell out of myself, but I can't deny that Melody makes me feel good about myself.

Is it wrong to keep her around? Definitely, but I can't let her go. She's everything I thought—no, scratch that—I know I need, and the unfortunate part of it all is I have to let her go. Sure, I'll live to regret it, but I'd rather hurt her now than to continue to string her along and have to break her heart when she finds out that Gaea and Kynsley have to be number one in my life.

Walking into her modest apartment has me feeling like public enemy number one. Her décor, which is happily mixed rusty and polished patinas, incorporates old- and new-world distinctions and fine and rough textiles. Everything's elegantly understated, melodiously hued, and happily feminine. When she answers the door, her warm smile and angelic face have me wondering if doing this in her home is a bad idea.

"Hey, babe!" she purrs as she pulls me in her warm embrace.

"Hey, Mel, how are you doing, love?" I croon out, placing a kiss on her forehead. If I'm not mistaken, she looks as if she has something plaguing her conscious as well. But being true to her stubborn self, she holds it in. I want to push her, but fate isn't on our side today. I know after I say what I need to say, we'll be no more. But the longer I hold her, it becomes apparent that letting her go will be a lot harder on me than I thought. I guess holding on to her for a bit longer won't hurt anything. I'll let her go after dinner. Yeah, that makes sense— after dinner. To lighten the mood, she picks up her camera and points it at me.

"Take your clothes off, Flash. Slowly." She winks for dramatic effect.

"Melody," I drag out.

"Quiet, it's for my private collection for *My. Pleasure. Only!*" she purrs out.

"You got me feeling like a little punk," I say as I pull the camera down.

"Flash, hush. You're going to ruin the moment. Live in the moment. Let your desire for me overpower your thoughts. Forget the camera is here. It's just me and you," she says as she winks.

Something flashes in her eyes for a brief second, and just like that, her eyes darken with lust. Most wouldn't have caught it, but I do.

"Mel, I'll do this but under one condition. You stop running from whatever this is that's growing between us," I say, confusing even myself. She isn't the one running; hell, I am. In my heart, I know I don't want her, but I also know that I'm tired of Gaea and her shit.

"Kwame, don't complicate things with thoughts on defining what we are doing here. Just live in the moment," she states.

"I mean, what are we doing here?" I ask, feeling completely curious at that exact moment.

"I want you and I to go public. I want the world to know that I am your woman," she purrs.

I go completely quiet and can see in her eyes that her heart's breaking. I guess it's become apparent why I'm quiet. I'm not sure about any of this. I don't want this with her; I want it with Gaea. Sure, I play coy, but even a blind man can see that she's fallen for me. How foolish have I been to not see the signs since I walked through her door? I'm giving her an out, but she's pleading with me to stay.

"You don't want this, do you, Flash? I'm so stupid. How could I fall for you, knowing you were vocal in not wanting us to be anything more than platonic?"

"You shouldn't have—"

"I shouldn't have what? Started falling in love with you? You're absolutely right. I had no business doing that. I had fun, and it was clear I should be doing something else because you for damn sure were. You think I'm stupid, but I know you're still in love with your baby mama. Anytime she calls, you cut our shit short. At first, I was cool with it because your baby has been through some shit. But I see now that I allowed you to use me!"

"Melody, wait, I never meant to hurt you. It's not what you're thinking. I was reckless with you, and I feel sorry that you're hurting. It's a lot I would like to tell you, but you wouldn't understand."

"Wouldn't understand what, Flash? That you were only using me to get to her? You know what? Here are your proofs and a little extra. Next time you think to contact me, do me a favor and just *don't*. I'm done with this!"

"Melody, wait..."

"No! You listen here, Flash. I was open with you. I was under-standing of your pain. I nursed and licked your wounds when you would come to my home pouting. I ignored smelling the perfume on your clothes because I know you co-parent with your baby mama. I held my tongue when you would shut down. I get that you two are close, but I refuse to stand around, longing for something you can't give me! I crave a love so deep from you that it moves heaven and earth, making the God's jealous! You can't give me those things. No, you refuse to give me those things! I don't want your pity! I want to know that someone's love for me is felt deep down in their soul, becoming a pillar of strength in their faith. I crave a love so pure that I *know* Christ created this man just for me, with eyes just for me, and a heart that's been dipped in gold and God's anointing just for *me*! I *deserve* that, and I refuse to settle for anything less! I was afraid too, but you know what? I had the courage to give you my heart willingly, even with a hell of a lot of faults. Just get out!"

"Wait, Melody! We can't end things like this. I promise to give you a fair chance. Let me take you out, love."

"I'll think about it. Now get the fuck out of my house!" she yells.

I'm anxiously aware of needing a moment to clear my head before I head back to the house to face Gaea. I call up Tobias to meet up with me at Amour Noir to have a drink. He gives me some pushback because, like everyone else, he's tired of the back-and-forth bullshit that Gaea and I are constantly going through. I just know he'll flip shit when he realizes that, despite his warning, I still went ahead and fucked around with Melody. I didn't think to ask if he's coming alone until I see him and Anais walk into the club together. From the look on her face, I know it's about to be some shit, and his ignorant ass smirks and shrugs as they make their way over to me. Before I could truly greet them both, Ana lights into my ass.

"You got some fucking nerve to be fucking a bitch that comes to my studio! She's been jaw jacking for weeks now about the way you fuck her. If she hadn't paid in full for a year's worth of lessons, I'd beat her ass, strictly based off the fact that she is well aware of who my niece and sister are! I know my sister has some fucked up ways, but you mad sloppy, my boy! You let that bitch get close to my babies, and you'll live to regret ever meeting me," she says before mushing my head and marching off toward the backstage area.

"You couldn't warn a nigga before Hurricane Ana stormed through?" I ask as we do the whole handshake shoulder-bump thing.

"You know how she is. There ain't no stopping her once she gets going. Just let her calm down a little bit. I'm sure she will get over it," he says while chuckling.

"So are y'all a thing or..." I trail off, fully expecting him to deny that they have something going on. I honestly don't get why they choose to keep everything so hush-hush. It isn't like the world can't see that there's something there with those two besides their *friendship*.

"Man, get you some business. Here it is, your life's all fucked, and you're worried about whether or not I'm digging Anais's guts out! You are something else," he says, cracking up, but I fail to see the humor in anything he's said.

"Just don't hurt her, aight!" I state in all seriousness. I know Tobias, and I know once he gets bored, he'll get rid of the relationship or whatever it is altogether.

"You mean like you're doing with her sister and Melody? Don't look so shocked that she knows, Flash. You forget, she was dealing with a habitual cheater for I don't know how many years. I'm sure she saw the signs. I watched the woman you proclaimed to love break down one night and get up the next morning to face the world head on like everything in the world is fine. She puts on a brave front for you and Kynsley, but she is broken. She smells the perfume and cleans the lipstick stains out of your shirts. Yes, she was wrong for hurting you, but she is valid in holding her heart until someone comes along that is worthy of it. Whether it is you or someone else, and honestly, right now, it's not you. You are feeding her fears by being everything she thought you would be. She needed you to fight, and you walked away. You jumped right into this thing with Melody, disregarding the fact that I warned you about messing with her, but you proceeded anyway. That woman is crazy, so know that I have absolutely no problem with checking her ass when it comes down to my niece and her mother," he declares.

"I won't even ask how you know. But she told me she's fallen in love with me."

"Nigga, in four weeks, you can't possibly believe that. Her ass ain't in love with you, especially since she's been... You know what? I'm going to let you cook. Because right now, you aren't thinking logically, like not at all. You want what's easy, but that's not how this shit works. You want Gaea to drop years of hurt to flat-out love you when you've been holding on to shit with Maxwell your whole life. Come on, bruh, be fair," he says while taking a sip of his vanilla crown and coke.

My thoughts take me back to the night before. Yesterday started great and just kept getting better. It wasn't just the way we reached a hot and sweaty explosion after fifteen minutes of me rhythmically sliding my dick in and out of Gaea's tight, sopping-wet pussy. It was the manner in which we kissed throughout the act and moaned together. We were genuinely happy in these moments, our guards completely down, just finished fully living in the moment.

My favorite moments happened when I whispered, "I love you so much," to Gaea, and her pussy muscles would grip me tighter. Her river would just about drown us, and she'd clamp her legs around me, connecting us by souls, and push back against me with more passion than my heart could stand.

When she said, "I love you, too," how my heart swelled, and my dick felt like it got harder, and I just wanted to stay inside her forever. Thinking of all that, I'm glad I'm was seated because my dick is growing.

My thoughts are halted when I look over to see Gaea embrace

some guy before she walks on the stage. I know I shouldn't be mad, because I have a whole woman I'm entertaining, but that shit pisses me off to the high heavens, especially when he cuffs her ass, and she winks at him. The difference is I haven't fucked Melody. Yeah, we kiss, and she sucked my dick a few times, but I never penetrated her. But Gaea and that nigga were embracing like they had history! A deep and intimate history. I knew I had Melody, but damn, she is living under my roof and still wasn't honest about her shit. I can't imagine, nor can I handle another man getting close to what I know is mine. I'm gonna check her hot ass for being out and embarrassing the fuck out of me.

"Chill, Flash. That's her old neighbor or some shit—well, rather her friend," Tobias informs me. He can sense that I'm about to show my naturally black ass up in this club with no valid reason; I'm the one that told her we couldn't be. Even with someone else on my arm, I expect her to fight harder than what she's been doing. Instead, she pulls back. I guess I can't fault her, knowing now she has great suspicions that I'm involved with someone else. I guess that's the purpose of being diligent in not only prayer but matters of the heart. My eagerness is literally blocking my blessings. It allows me to see what I want to see and blinds my vision to what's right under my nose.

I can't see Gaea's actions, because I'm so tied up on the words that were spoken. When in reality, she has committed to me in unspoken terms. She lives in my home, mothered my daughter, cooks my food, cleans my home, started volunteering for my charities, washes my clothes, and gives me benefits no other man can ever say they had. Well, one could, but if he knows what's best for him, he won't mumble a word about it. Yet my anger keeps me so hyper focused on the fact that she's hurt my pride. She isn't bending in the manner that I want her too. I'm starting to think that maybe if I had taken a moment to breathe, I would've realized that people love differently and at different speeds. Past hurts hinder and blind us from seeing what we actually need. I guess I'm as guilty as Gaea in this instance for protecting my heart.

She steps onto the stage, wearing an all-black, open mesh dress

58

from Bebe paired with the Ricki Bow strap sandal. My girl looks so fucking good, and it's taking everything in me to not run on stage and snatch her off. She has my dick about to pop my zipper when she turns around to greet the band and reveals an open back, showing bare skin from nape to waist. Her face is lightly made up with her plump lips painted a beautiful crimson. I love seeing her in this element. Here she is, so free and confident in who she truly is as a person. Yes, she loves nursing, but this is her calling.

How did we ever lose our way
And try to say love is a losing game?
Should've never tried to play.
Bring your love on back to me.
Stop this insanity
Before we go too far.

When she opens her mouth to sing "Insanity" by Gregory Porter and Lalah Hathaway, I swear I fall deeper in love with her. I make the decision then and there to let Melody go. I pull out my phone, take a picture along with a video, and caption it: My Beautiful Gypsy.

I'm deliberately telling the world she's mine. I don't care if she doesn't agree. If her heart is meant to be mine, she'll jump in line. Almost instantaneously, all of my social media handles are going crazy.

Mel: So you left me to go be with this basic ass bitch?

Watch ya fucking mouth Mel. That's my daughter's mother!

Mel: Nah nigga I said what I said! You are so trifling. You're the worst kind of fuckboy. One that genuinely think he's good. You will pay for breaking my heart!

I immediately close my texting app. I have no energy to go back and forth with her. Arguing with her is fruitless when I know deep down I'm letting her ass go. Tuning back in to the raspy rendition of the song has me wondering if this song is possibly for me. The lyrics hit too close to home, so it just has to be for me.

We were lovers
And the best of friends.
And I hope, I hope that we can be that

Until the end.
Sometimes the lover
Can be angry 'til the end.
But it's always the friend inside
That will make amends.

"Gaea, why didn't you tell me you were performing? Where is Kynsley?" I walk up on her, firing off questions before she can get back to the nigga I saw her hugging.

"Kyns is fine. She's with Mom and Kalyse. I left instructions for Kion to stay with them. Miquel is here with me. As for your other question, when would I have had time? You're always gone with what I am assuming is your girlfriend, so I didn't feel the need to bother you with anything I have going on. Now if you'd excuse me, I need to speak with Drexel here," she says before turning to walk toward a dark-skinned brother. All I see is red when I walk over to the both of them.

"Aye, my man, wrap this up; I need to speak to my child's mother!" I bark out at them and become enraged when the nigga laughs at me.

"Man, you are funny as hell. The fact that you tried to slide that you are Kynsley's father up in there is funny as fuck. But, ummm, because I respect Gaea's fine ass, I'm gonna walk away instead of checking yo' ass for stepping to me wrong. I'm letting you get a pass this time. Next time, you won't be so lucky. I'm going to go holla at Ana to let you continue to stake your claim. Aye, Bug, I'll holla at you later," Drexel says as he kisses her cheek.

"My nigga, that jaw jacking will get yo' ass fucked up! My claim was already staked when I moved her and our daughter in my home. That fine ass muthafucka standing right there is off-limits," I declare.

"Nigga, again, I'm going to let yo' ass cook out of respect for my girl. Shit mad platonic. If things were what you saying they are, you wouldn't be clowning, now would you?"

I go to chin check his ass, but Tobias steps in. He always makes his presence known when I'm about to lose my cool and fuck shit up. Sometimes, I appreciate it, but in this moment, I don't. I don't give a fuck who buddy is, but he's about to feel my rage.

"I told yo' ass to be cool, but you just had to start some shit. Drex, go on over there with Ana. Y'all niggas make too much fucking money to be acting like some bitches up in this club!" Tobias states.

"Man, fuck that nigga!" I say while grabbing a hold of Gaea's arm, dragging her to the restroom. I make sure the coast is clear before I lock the door to go off on her ass. I don't care how crazy I look.

"Why the fuck you talking to other niggas about Kynsley?" I spit out.

"First off, Kwame, don't come over here with your nose all flared and ya chest all puffed out, talking shit. You rolling up on Drex, like that was unnecessary. You were completely out of line. That's my friend. The only friend I had while I was in Jackson. Strictly platonic! But why am I explaining anything to you when you got a whole fucking situation going on!" she asks, attempting to leave the restroom.

"Nah, don't think you get to speak your peace and then dismiss me. You talking about that man yo' friend, but I saw him grip yo' ass before you hit the stage. Stop trying to play me, Gaea!" I yell.

"You said all of that but still have yet to acknowledge or address the shit about your bitch," she says, tossing her hand in my direction.

"Yo, watch yo' hands! I ain't addressing it, because it ain't shit to address!"

"Kwame, get out of my way. I'm not doing this with you tonight! I've been through this shit before, and I refuse to do it with you! We full on live together and share a whole fucking bed every time you bring yo' egg-head ass home. I look over the shit you do because I'm aware I hurt you, but I'm not about to keep giving in to your tantrums and punishing myself when you do what you want to do!" she yells out on the verge of crying.

"Melody doesn't mean shit the me. All I've ever wanted was you, but you keep pushing me away! There is no reason to be where wc are!"

"Yes the fuck there is, and her name is Melody! Thank you for finally being honest about your shit! Listen to everything I'm about to say, and take it as you take the bible! I'm not fucking with any man in my life who plays house with me, getting full-on wife privileges and knowingly fucks another bitch, never bothering to be honest with me! I was praying that yo' extra-wack ass forgave me, but I no longer fucking care! As of tomorrow, Kynsley and I will move into a home! I'm done playing house with yo' ass," she says with tears cascading down her cheeks.

"Gypsy!" I lower my voice. I never thought my actions would hurt her in the manner in which they do. But truth is, they did. Here she is, pouring her heart out to me, showing me that she clearly has some love for me. This shit is painful. I can't catch my breath, and my grown ass is crying too. I'm losing the woman I love for a woman I liked. I can't fucking handle it. "If you walk out of that door, I'll never forgive you!"

"I'm not the one that needs forgiveness. Goodbye, Flash," she says while wiping her face and storming out.

CHAPTER 11

Janet

*H*aving children was never a part of my plan in terms of my life with Theodore. It was always something that he desired—hell, something he required in order for me to be his wife. At first, I thought he would eventually get over having children until I went through his office and saw he was going to divorce my ass. He had somehow found that I had been aborting his seeds the entire length of our three-year marriage. I seduced his ass that night and became pregnant with Anais.

Lord knows I can't stand that little bitch. Her mouth is too fucking smart, and when she discovered she could whoop my ass, that hate grew deep.

Now Gaea, although I didn't want her ass either, I could easily manipulate her to do what I wanted her to do. That was until she let Anais get in her head and warp her thinking on me and help her secure a bag. She had it all laid out for her; all she had to do was stick to the plan.

The plan is so solid that I pray that I won't have to walk around afraid that Teddy will find out that I'm fucking everyone I come into contact with. Hell, I've been fucking, and when I was pregnant, nothing brought me to an orgasm faster than knowing that another nigga was spilling his kids on mine. It's some sick shit to think that way, but I'm not your average bitch. I have been very careful with my shit until I started fucking Maxine. That bitch became clingy and expected me to only fuck with her.

She has to be crazy as hell to think I'm not bouncing my ass all over my husband's dick! Despite what she believes, I'm not leaving Teddy for anybody. I'm going to collect that coin from Maxine's ass and go on about my business. Well, that was the plan until her stupid ass son became so fucking sloppy with his shit. He fucks anything walking because he knows I can talk Gaea into doing anything I need her to do. Well, at least until he got that damn girl pregnant. Gaea jumped ship. He's lucky she didn't for real shoot his ass. She has been telling us for the longest that she was sick of him walking all over her heart.

When she came to me a few months after they split up and told me she was pregnant, I was happy because that meant the merger that Ted thought nobody knew about could proceed. But no, the little hoe had to go and fuck Kwame and get pregnant. Knowing she was pregnant, her ass had to go, so we moved her two hours away. All I had to do was throw some of this good pussy at Theodore, and he broke his neck to hide her ass. It all worked until she started to miss home, and I fell in love with Kynsley. Right, the woman who didn't want kids fell in love with that little girl the moment I laid eyes on her in the neonatal intensive care unit.

"Janet, I've given you all the time in the world to persuade Ted to change his mind. While your pussy is good, it is for damn sure not worth millions! Give me one good reason I shouldn't peal your scalp?"

"Jeff, let's stop right there. Regardless of when I deliver, know that it will get done. Know that regardless of when I deliver, you still gonna try to beat down these walls."

"Don't flatter yourself, Janet. It was never you I wanted. Only the money. You forget I'm married to your best friend. Regardless of us fucking around, I'll never leave her!"

"You act like that's what I'm asking you to do. Boy, pluh-ease, your wife is a lipstick lesbian. She more concerned with bumping pussies than she is fucking you. Please tell me, when was the last time she fucked you? Hmmmm, let's try three fucking years ago!" I spit out.

Before I know what's happening, Jeffery grabs me by my throat and shoves his dick in my wet pussy. I know the buttons to push to get what I need. Yes, I ratted Maxine out; I only omitted the fact that I was the reason the bitch was now dabbling in the lady pond. I caught her at a moment of weakness, taught that bitch to eat pussy, and we've been fucking around ever since.

"Your mouth has always been a problem for me," he says as he strokes my g-spot.

"You two muthafuckas are so fucking ridiculous! Jeffery, here you are, in our home, fucking this bitch, and raw at that! You wonder why I won't fuck you!" Maxine shouts as she barges into the room, swinging her bat. She could've at least let me get my nut off before she knocked that nigga upside his head.

"Wait a minute, baby, I can explain," he says, ducking and dodging her swings, dick slanging everywhere.

"Maxine, put the fucking bat down. We can stop hiding the shit. Get over here and eat Mama's pussy!" I demand, and first she lifts an eyebrow at me before she puts the bat down. She crawls over to me and starts to run her velvety tongue all over my folds, catching every drop of my nectar.

"You two bitches have been fucking, huh?" Jeff asks while stroking his dick.

"Instead of doing all that fucking talking, put that dick to use and join us!" I moan out as she increases the speed of her licks, paying special attention to my clit.

You would've sworn he had gotten his hands on those millions he's had his eyes on. He struts across the room, removes Maxine's thong, and enters her in one beautiful stroke. As he dives into her, Maxine flicks her tongue in and out of my pussy walls, sucking the nut right out of me. As Jeff continues to fuck the shit out of Maxine, I grab my vibrator out of my bag and go to work on my own pussy.

On the brink of an orgasm, I find my vibrator is now replaced with Jeffery's dick. He pulls me on top and places Maxine on his face. As he's giving me everything he's got, Maxine takes a handful of my hair and starts fucking my mouth until we all cum in unison. Shortly after, we all come down off our highs, and I'm getting dressed to head home. I think it'll be best to let them soak up the moment and get back to them because after tonight, I'm done with both of their asses. This shit has gone on for too long and playing too close to home. I can't lose my husband behind these two idiots, so I know walking out this door, I'll more than likely have to kill them both.

"You have five days, Janet! If I don't have it by then, people are going to start dying," he says as he cuddles closer to Maxine. I chuckle because he has no idea that they'll be the only two people to die.

CHAPTER 12

Maxwell

*T*here are things that never sound good coming from another man, and the sentence, "Your hoe ass wife is the reason our granddaughter went missing," is probably at the top of the list of things not to say. I get the rap of being a bad guy, and by all means, I am, but I'm not about to snitch on that hoe for being a hoe without implicating my involvement with her. Nope. What I'm gonna do is present the information to Kwame and his mother to let them decide what to do with it. For the longest, I was able to do what I wanted to do without repercussions, but this time, I want to try a different approach. But first, I need to handle my business here with Karen.

"Hey, Karen, thanks for agreeing to meeting with me. Before you begin, I would like to apologize to you for damaging our children. I let my hurt and disdain for you grow like the cancer it is and ultimately cause the breakdown in the pain my children have felt as a whole," I say.

"Maxwell, I never thought I would hear those words from you. What's bringing them out? You aren't dying, are you?"

"Every day, but not too soon. Once Kynsley went missing, I began to think about the real possibility of growing old alone. My anger behind you and James has haunted me for twenty-six years. I loved you, Karen; in my own unique way, I did. I didn't nurture it in the manner it should've been nurtured, but I tried."

"James and me? What exactly do you think happened, Max?" Karen asks, looking seemingly perplexed.

"Karen, it's been years. You can finally admit that you two had a thing," I state, growing irritated with the direction this conversation is headed in.

"Maxwell, I'll admit I did sleep with James. But we were much more than that. I loved you so much, but you broke me, and he was there to put me back together. When the kids needed things, and you flat-out refused, he was there. When you seemed to get your stuff together, I would drop him. To be honest, I don't know if Kalyse was yours or not, because James was heavily in the picture at that time. In fact, he's still here. He's just been playing in the shadows."

"Karen, what the fuck do you mean, you don't know if she's my daughter or not?" I growl out.

"Exactly what I said. You thought the way you did me wouldn't have any repercussions? Hardly. You may have been a hoe, but I was a calculated one. I did what was necessary so that my children could survive," she says nonchalantly.

Here I am, coming here prepared to apologize, but I'm hit with another gut punch. All this time, I thought I was in the wrong, but her ass is just as wrong. But Kalyse just has to be mine; she looks identical to Kynsley, and she's for sure a Jacobsen. I can't stand to see her face, so I leave. I'll have to pass this information on to Kwame another day. As for now, I have some shit to figure out, starting with getting a paternity test for my daughter.

A few days later.

Tobias is the closest person to Kwame, so I figure it'll be best if I drop what I have in his lap. I'm a force in my own right, but if I team up with someone else, then we'll be unstoppable. I know deep down that Janet's ass has to be stopped. She's becoming dangerous. I can't have her sinking her claws in my son, not when his trifling ass mother and I had already doomed him In ways that wasn't repairable.

"Max, I'm going to be honest with you here. I was skeptical about meeting with you. It's no secret that I don't like you. But I will say after looking into some of this, I'm shocked."

"Shocked at what, per-say? The fact that Janet is shady or the fact that I was fucking her?" I ask nonchalantly.

"Neither of those are shockers. That shit is just gross. You fuck anything though, man. But this whole Maxine and Janet is a filthy ass mess. Those two bitches are married to the most powerful men in this city, aside from my father, so excuse me for being baffled at this whole plot. They could've at least made their anger believable. Maxine, OK, yeah, I can believe it. But Janet? Nah, that bitch is just Satan in a blue dress," he states.

"So what do you suppose we do?" I ask.

"We are going to hit that bitch where it hurts. Her fucking pockets!"

"You mean to tell me you got that much power, but you couldn't stop me from fucking with ya boy?"

"Maxwell, don't push it. I'll still beat yo' ass, bruh," he says, standing from behind his desk.

"Aight, calm down, killa! But I need to ask you a favor, and I need you to keep it from Kwame."

"Depends on what it is," he states flatly.

"I need a paternity test done for Kalyse and I," I say.

"Excuse me? I need you to repeat yourself because I know I didn't hear you correctly! Kalyse is a teenager. Why now? It's not like you've ever been on child support for her. Hell, if we are being honest, Mr. James has picked up your slack plenty of times."

"What do you mean, picked up my slack?" I ask, angry all over again.

"Look, man, I've already said to much. Kalyse is good, and you are striving to change your life. Let's not open a can of worms to ruin two lives in the process."

"Tobias, what you don't realize is that James was my best friend. I may have been wrong about doing my dirt, but Kalyse doesn't deserve to continue living a lie. Too many men get suckered like that and then leave their daughters looking for a broken replica of the man that hurt them. If you don't do this for any other reason, then do it for her. She deserves it," I state.

"Alright, man, I'll see what I can do, but I won't make any promises. This shit is going to change the way your children look at their mother, and I don't want any parts of that portion of it. Being that Mr. James is actually a good dude to your children, I'll get the answers you seek," he says noncommittally.

"Thanks, Tobias. I appreciate this, man," I say as I walk out of his office to head out to the bar to drown myself in a bottle of Bourbon. All the bad I've done in my lifetime is catching up with me, and call me a bitch, but I can't handle it.

CHAPTER 13

Gaea

Kwame's really done with me. In fact, he's avoiding me at all costs. Aside from the time we spend together for Kynsley's sake, we hardly speak. Hell, not even then. We basically talk through and around Kynsley. The shit hurts, and I have no one to blame for it but myself. Well, not really because that nigga was lying to me. But prior to our fallout, I was to blame. He'd shown me time and time again how much he cared for me, but I was too tied up in my past hurts to appreciate him.

Losing him a second time woke me up to what he was trying to get me to see. For years, he stayed by my side when shit would go wrong with Aaron and me. He never complained about the times he literally had to pick me up off the ground and nurse my fragile heart back to good health. He just did it. No questions asked, he showed me time and time again, but I continued to shit on his efforts.

So now I'm forced to sit here in Amour Noir, watching him give another what should be mine. I have to put on this brave face, knowing that when I get back to the house, I'll want to put his face through a wall. I tried to move out, but his ass blocked it at every bend. He doesn't want me but doesn't want me to move on. What kind of psycho shit is that? I feel like part of that is tied up in his emotions about Drexel.

Drex is cool and all, but he isn't for me. That nigga is a mean ass bully, straight out of Jackson, Mississippi. He only has a soft spot for Kynsley and me because she checked him one day for parking too close to her swing set. Kwame is just being crazy for no reason when he's still out there doing his fucking dirt. I want to bust him in his shit for embarrassing me the way that he did! But I can't. Not yet anyway. Not when I still haven't told him my dumb ass fucked around and let him get me pregnant. Yeah, baby number two by this man, and I'm nowhere near being his wife. Hell, I'm not even his girlfriend. I'm straight baby mama status. Ain't that some shit?

"Gaea, stop staring at them. Both of y'all are aggravating as fuck. He is fucking with that bum ass bitch to make you mad. In the beginning, you didn't treat him right, so let him find his happiness," Ana says.

"I'm not in the mood for your shit. I'll stop watching him when you admit that you have real feelings for Tobias. I know y'all are fucking. But I also know you're afraid to explore things with him," I counter.

"Ya know what? Handle your business, and I'll mind mine," she says while downing the rest of her lemon drop.

I glance back over at Kwame and his bootleg Regina Hall lookalike, and he lifts his glass to acknowledge me. Bastard. I lift my glass of water, smooth down my dress, and head toward the stage. Tonight, I know I look good, so if Kwame isn't catching what I'm pitching, then someone will. Simple logic, right?

Nah, I'm just gassing. I'll more than likely take my ass home and curl up with some butter pecan ice cream and binge watch seasons one and two of *Insecure*. I take a moment to make sure everything is intact and well put together so I'm not out here looking crazy. Tonight, I'm dressed in a rose-gold sequin slip dress with some nude sling backs. Lately, my makeup has been understated because my glow is real.

"Sistas, how y'all feeling? Brothers, are ya alright?" I speak directly into the mic. "I know it has been a good little minute since I've been on this stage. I came up here fully prepared to sing my heart out about how some man broke my heart. But I knew that wasn't the best route, because I broke my own heart and his as well. Then I thought about focusing on the fact I have been reunited with my daughter. You know, sing a song full of joy. But neither would ring true in explaining the inner turmoil I'm feeling right now. Sistas and brothers, I'm here to say if you have someone special in your life that sees the beauty in you, cherish it before a cleanup woman swoops in and takes what's rightfully yours," I say, looking in the direction of Kwame and the woman who's now rubbing his back.

He looks over at her like she's sprouted a second head. I swallow the lump that has developed in my throat as I wait for the piano to pour in for a few beats before I join in with the acoustic guitar. I clear my vision of the two of them and look at the crowd behind them instead. When I find my pace to the music, I open my mouth to sing right to Kwame's heart. Hopefully, by the end, it will open the doors of communication to hold a conversation.

I pretend that I'm glad you went away,
But these four walls close in more every day.
And I'm dying inside, and nobody knows it but me.
Like a clown, I put on a show.
The pain is real even if nobody knows.
And I'm crying inside, and nobody knows it but me.
Why didn't I say the things I needed to say?

About midway through the song, I see Kwame and his mystery woman begin to battle it out. They eventually get up and head toward the exit together. My heart shatters into a million pieces, but I continue to push through not only this song but my entire thirty-minute set. In some songs, I rejoice, while others make me feel like shit. I have a love so great that despite the hell we go through, it makes me see us for what we truly are—two imperfect people giving each other the chance to love freely and unapologetically flawed at times. To know that I've experienced that type of love but didn't hold on to it delicately and lost it was a lot to hold in. I make my exit from the stage and fell immediately into the warm bosom of my sister's embrace and cried.

"Butterfly, it's OK. Had I known you were going to do that, I would've advised against it. I know you realized the mistake you've made, but baby, sometimes, that just isn't enough. Use this as a tool to grow and to know what not to do for the next man," Anais says while rubbing my back, trying to ease the pain I feel.

"There won't be a next man, but OK. I get what you're saying. Let me go and thank Anthony and Brielle for allowing me to grace their stage again," I say as I turn to address Kion. "Kion, you stay. I'm certain you know the club like the back of your hand. If anything was to happen, I'm sure you would be there quicker than a moth to a flame. Please give me these few moments in private."

He nods his head but continues to move where he can see me and get to me if something were to happen. On my way to say thanks, I figure I need to relieve my screaming bladder, so I quickly step in and handle my business. The moment I step out of the restroom, I feel a piece of cold steel pressed against my back.

"Don't you dare fucking scream! If you scream, I'm going to blow your goddamn brains out."

"You don't have to do this. Whatever it is you want, I can give it to you," I say, searching the room with my eyes for Kion. Inside, I start to panic because I'm not able to get a clear visual on my team. I listen to what the voice behind the gun has to say.

"You see, I thought you were giving in and leaving Kwame alone after you got your daughter back. No, you continue further, bedding yourself deeper into his life. I don't like that one bit. My man isn't fond of it either," she snarls out.

"Lisette?"

"Yes, bitch, don't say my fucking name!"

"You don't have to do this. I'm not with Kwame. We are just parenting. Strictly parenting! Nothing more, nothing less. I promise if you let me go, I will go away. I will never come back," I plead.

"Bitch, it's too late. He loves you!" she yells out.

"No, he doesn't. He's moved on. He's dating. You can have your chance. I promise you I won't interfere."

"Look, bitch, just shut up. You're making my head hurt. Just walk toward the fucking exit. Don't do anything stupid, because I can and will kill you. I should shoot your ass anyway for fucking up my face," she says while turning to take a look at her face in the two-way mirror we're passing. I take that as an opportunity to turn and knock the gun out of her hand. As she watches the gun glide across the floor, I kick her dead in the middle of her chest. For once, I'm thankful I wore these heavy ass multi-eastern-art backhand straw grain Dr. Martens.

"You stupid bitch!" she yells out while struggling to catch her breath. I kick her a few times before I turn to run. I don't make it far before I'm yanked back by my hair.

"That'll be enough of that," I hear a deep Barry White baritone sternly say into my ear. I feel the hairs stand up on my arms because there is just no fucking way he's put me through all this hell. "You and Anais have always been a thorn in my side. Ana, because that bitch is a hoe but wouldn't fuck with me. A picky hoe—now ain't that some shit. But you... I thought you were different. You gave my son a whiff of that pussy and inadvertently screwed me out of millions when you couldn't play your part. You left him and fucked up my money! So if you know what's best for you, you'd get your ass in gear and follow me out of this club."

"Mr. Williamson! It's been you all this time? My father trusted you! He's saved your ass countless times! Why would you repay him like this?" I ask, clearly confused. All this time, I've been blaming innocent people when it's been this asshole the whole time. I just don't get this damn family. What the fuck is wrong with them?

"Stop asking all these questions and walk!" he growls.

"Boo, she fucked my face up again!" Lisette groans.

"Bitch, do you think I give a fuck about your face right now? You better hope we didn't lose time. Grab your gun and let's get the fuck up out of here!"

"Drop the gun, old man!" Kion bellows, shooting Li.

"You think your big ass scare me?" he asks, letting out a menacing laugh. "I'll light this bitch up, and we will all go out guns a blazing."

"Let her go! If it's money that you want, I can get you that!" I hear Kwame yell as he runs up on us.

"My nigga, you got $75 million laying around? You haven't been in the league that long. Ya money ain't long enough to let this bitch go. I'll take her off your hands so you can get another one."

"My daughter needs her mother, and I need my wife!" Kwame growls. What the fuck is he even talking about? We are barely even talking, and he is telling a nigga with a gun in his hand that has lost all of his marbles that I'm his wife.

"Wife? You married this nigga, Butterfly? You just insist on fucking up the church's money, don't you?"

"Again, Mr. Williamson, why?" I ask, completely ignoring his questions.

"Butterfly, look. Your father and I were supposed to acquire Martin Pharmaceuticals after you and Aaron were to graduate college. But you and Aaron didn't quite make it. Y'all went through that little spat, and he shelved it. I was certain that you two would get over y'all bullshit, but Teddy thought otherwise. All of that became evident and permanently shelved when he discovered you were pregnant, and Aaron wasn't the father. That's when this bird brain here waltzed into my life. She claimed that Kwame broke her heart, and you were the reasoning behind it. Had I known she couldn't whoop yo' ass, not even with a fucking gun, I would've left her ass alone a long time ago," he grumbles out as he aims his gun at her and shoots her four times—once in the head, twice in the heart, and once in the pussy. Once I see her brain matter splattered all over the floor, I violently vomit.

"Damn, that felt good. That bitch was annoying, and her pussy was trash. Gaea, you better watch that throwing up shit! These are $1,500 shoes," he says while yanking me by my hair. "Where was I? OK, so your trifling ass mammy convinced Aaron and I that you were pinning that little girl on Kwame because you were mad at Aaron for getting Yasmin pregnant. After Sidney was born, I killed Yasmin so there was no way for her to come back and interfere with you all. Only we didn't count on Teddy to be as smart as he was when it came to you girls. He kept you hidden but in broad daylight. It seemed like every time Janet would come close to telling Maxine where you were, Teddy would step in. That's when I found the evidence that Kynsley didn't belong to Aaron but was indeed Kwame's. Teddy got wind of me snooping, and he was adamant and ruthless with his practices. He cut ties and years of friendship and brotherhood off with me. That nigga is my frat, and he refuses to have any dealings with me because of some shit that went down between you and my son!" he yells.

"Look, man, let her go! You are mad at the wrong somebody! I'll get Theodore down here so y'all can talk! Just let her go!" Kwame yells as he continues to inch toward me.

"Nah, I'd rather not," he says while pulling me by my hair.

The next thing I know, I'm being shoved out of the way, and my scalp is on fire from my hair being pulled out. Everything starts moving in slow motion as I yell out to both Kwame and Jeffrey, "Stop! Don't let him shoot me! I'm pregnant!"

The pow from the gun is the last thing I hear before everything goes black.

CHAPTER 14

Kwame

"I'm pregnant!" That shit keeps playing on repeat in my head. There's no way that the woman I so desperately love is going to be taken from me like this. How can it be that just an hour before, she was showing me her heart? Granted, I was here with someone else, I felt every single note of that song. I need her to know that I still care, that I still want the same things that she does. But it seems as if life is never on our side. But just this once, I pray that God will grant His mercy on us and give us time to get it right. He just has to. Kynsley needs her mother, and I need to make good on my word and make her my wife. Gaea is it for me.

"Kion, kill him! I don't give a country fuck how you do it; just get it done!" I growl out as I jump in my Yukon to follow the ambulance to the hospital. I pick up the phone to call Theodore to inform him of what's happening.

"Yo, Pops! You need to get down to the hospital now. Gaea was shot, and I don't know how this is going to turn out."

"What the hell do you mean, Gaea was shot!" he yells.

"Long story short, it was Jeffery this whole fucking time. Ana is in the ambulance with her and I'm trying to keep up. I got to go," I say, ending the call and tossing my phone in the passenger seat. I turn on my hazard lights and put the pedal to the metal to get to my girl before it is too late. If she survives this with my child still in the cushiness of her womb, then I'll marry her as soon as she's able to utter the words "I Do."

I rush into the hospital and head straight to the nurses' station. I let them know that absolutely under no circumstances should anyone other than the medical staff and family know anything about what is going on with Gaea and her case. I put in a call to my team and give them a quick run-down on the events of the night. The police are swarming around the hospital, eager to get a statement from Ana and me, but I refuse to let them get anything out of either of us until we have updates on Gaea.

"You bitch! Why the fuck did you bring her here? This is her goddamn fault!" Ana says, jumping across chairs in the waiting room and knocking the shit out of Janet.

"Anais, enough!" Theodore shouts as I look on at Anais now choking the shit out of her mother.

"Pops, this is one time you might want to let that be! Had your wife not been feeding the Williamson family bullshit, my wife and unborn child wouldn't be here fighting for their lives. We would be living our life in dysfunctional bliss right now!" I state as I signal my security detail to break up the beat down happening across the room from us. I know I probably shouldn't have let Ana beat her mom's ass, but if she didn't do it, I would've strangled that bitch with her toe nails. I swear I can't fathom being that low down and evil. I still don't get her aim in all of this. What can you stand to gain when you're putting your daughter's life in danger? Like I legit don't get that at all. You single-handedly orchestrated bullshit that's going to stick with and affect my girls for the rest of their lives, and I can't rock with that.

"What do you mean, wife and unborn child? Furthermore, what the fuck does Janet have to do with Gaea being shot!" Theodore's voice booms out.

"You told that bitch to stop fucking with that damn family altogether, but she didn't! She had been feeding that family bullshit for *years* in regard to Kynsley and Gaea. She had them thinking that she was biologically Aaron's daughter. She was feeding the beast. Had she not done that shit, my sister wouldn't be back there fighting to live! All she ever wanted was your approval and your love, but you're too sick in the fucking head to see that. From this moment going forward, you're dead to me. Y'all better pray that she pulls through because if she doesn't, I'm gonna be at your fucking head every time I see her. I swear on my soul, I'll kill her ass!" Ana says before Tobias picks her up and whispers something in her ear. Whatever he's saying calms her little ass down. I look back over at Theodore, and I swear I've never seen him so mad.

"To answer the questions that were directed at me. First, I didn't know about the baby until she was shot. The last thing I heard her say was *I'm pregnant*. Now, either you offer your blessing and allow me to marry her, or I do it anyway without your consent. Either way, it's going to happen. For so long, we have allowed outside forces to navigate the love we had between us. But no more; we are going to take control of our own destiny. Also, going forward, your wife is to have no contact with my family. She is a threat to their safety and a cancer in their lives. I hope you understand and respect the choices I've made on their behalf," I state.

"Janet, is any of what they are saying true?" Theodore asks.

"Before you jump to assume shit, allow me the luxury of having the benefit of the doubt. Let me explain. I'm sure they have some of this information mixed up!" Janet snaps.

"You've said enough! Get the fuck out of here and pray I don't snap your fucking neck! You better have all of your shit out of my house before I find the strength to come back," he says while exiting to go check on Ana and to check with the nurses for any updates.

To add insult to injury, Melody shows her ass up to the hospital because the news is reporting that I'm here with my girlfriend. When I say she's showing her natural black ass, I mean she's cut a fucking fool. She has no valid reason to be here. We broke things off over dinner when she decided it would be a great idea to show up at Gaea's set. Yeah, I was mad at Gaea, but I wouldn't purposely disrespect her by bringing someone who was temporary all up in her space. That's just flat-out disrespectful.

"Bitch, I know you didn't just waltz your ass up in here disrespecting my sister as she is fighting for her life! Now, see, I've already whooped one hoe ass tonight behind my sister; don't let yo' ass be the next to catch this fade!" Ana yells while squaring up to fight.

"I'm here to support my man!" Melody counters.

Pop! "Wrong answer, bitch!" *Pop! Pop!* "I don't give a fuck if you was here to see yo' wrinkled ass great grandpappy; don't disrespect my sister!" *Pop!* Melody proves to be no match for Anais. But then again, nobody is. That girl is a beast in riding her own lane. She has Melody by her hair, delivering a clean-cut fade.

"Ana, let me handle this!" I grumble. Almost instantaneously, she focuses her sights on me and drops Melody like the rag doll she is. *Pop!*

"Muthafucka, you better teach your bitches their place! I frankly don't give a fuck what the bitch is to you, just don't let this hoe cross that line again! I'm tempted to beat yo' ass, but Tobias told me to chill. Get rid of that hoe before I end up on the first forty-eight!" she says before she storms off in the direction her father disappeared in earlier.

"Melody, get yo' ass up! Why the fuck would you come up here? I have enough going on without you adding to it! What part of I'm done with your ass prompted you to come up here?" I growl out.

"Baby, I didn't think you were serious. We can work this out!" she croaks out.

"Mel, ain't no working this out. It was nothing to begin with! You knew what the fuck you were doing when you convinced me to meet you at Amour Nior," I say, growing heated. All this bitch has for me is the audacity—*the audacity*—to further fuck up my day!

"She needed to see you are happy with me!" she explains.

"No, muthafucka, I'm not! Gaea is it for me! You're so misinformed. I'm not trying to be your man. Hell, I'm not. We were just having fun. I'm sorry if I led you on. I'm a fucked-up person for that, but you had to know that coming up here wouldn't be good! I'm asking you as nicely as I can to stay away from my family!" I yell, signaling my crew to get this bitch the fuck out of my face! I have enough to deal with, and dealing with her shenanigans isn't a top priority.

"Flash, you haven't seen the last of me! On my mama, you'll regret fucking me over!" she yells as Kion carries her out.

"I told you not to fuck with that bitch! Now I have to play cleanup, Kwame, and I hate playing fucking cleanup. My name ain't Betty Wright, my nigga! That bitch is gonna be a problem; mark my words!" Tobias says.

Five Days Later.

"Where am I? Is my baby OK?" Gaea croaks out, feeling around the bed to make sure everything is still intact.

"Calm down, Gypsy. All three of you are just fine. We just need you to rest. I'll have the doctor come in and explain everything to you once I get what I have to say off my chest," I plead with her. If she'll give me half a chance, I'll wipe all of the bad away and love her so hard it would shake up heaven and earth. We just have to work. We've been through too much shit not to work at all. My biggest blessings are wrapped up in her. God brought her back to me, and with me is where she'll stay. I can't wait to start life brand new with her. I just need her to say yes, like yesterday. We can wash away the past and get right back to loving each other. Fuck a Melody, and for damn sure, fuck a Drexel!

"Three? What the hell are you talking about, Kwame?" she asks, panicking.

"Gypsy, we are having twins." I chuckle. "But before you speak, I want you to know that everything you were trying to convey to me while you were on that stage and singing you heart out, I felt. I've loved you since the day you dumped that God-awful blueberry tea in my lap. I've chased you for your love for years, and I would like to keep that love for a million more. Even though I've been mad and often times stubborn, my love for you has never wavered. Why else did you think I would have you in my home, our home? I needed you near because having half of you was better than not having you at all. You and our children, both born and unborn, mean the world to me. I meant what I said when I called you my wife. You are it for me, Gaea, and I pray like hell you feel I am it for you. Please don't let that ring on your finger be in vain. Please take me out of my misery and say you will be my wife! Will you marry me, Gypsy?"

I see the moment her eyes spot her fourteen-karat white-gold Vera Wang four-carat diamond twist engagement ring. The tears form and start to cascade down her cheeks. I know that she wants to say something; I just don't know what it'll be. I walk over to her bed, and she pulls me close, giving me the most disgusting, sweetest kiss I could've ever gotten. Disgusting because her ass hasn't brushed her teeth since forever but sweetest because I take that as a yes. But I need her to say it. I need her to vocally admit that she wants this as much as I do.

"Kwame, it would be my honor to be your wife," her raspy voice calls out as tears flow down her cheeks.

"Like right now?" I ask.

"Kwame, you can't be serious."

"Oh, but I am. I don't need you changing your mind on me," I say as I push the button to signal my pastor to come in.

"We don't even have a marriage certificate," she argues.

"I took care of that two days ago. I will give you the wedding you deserve later; I just need you to marry me today. We've run from each other so long because people decided to play puppeteers with our love and pollute it with their secrets and lies. The pastor is right outside of this room along with our families. Let's do this, babe," I plead.

"OK..."

"I know it seems... wait? You said OK?"

"Yes, let's do this, Flash!"

"Great, but do me a favor?"

"What's that?"

"Never call me Flash." I chuckled.

Who would've thought that a bullet would be the reason to make us get our shit together? By far, this feels like the best option for me and my girls. Our journey certainly hasn't been pretty, but it has definitely been worth the wait. Hearing her say she'll be mine forever has a nigga feeling all good inside. Now I just need to handle this Jeffery shit before I can breathe easy.

CHAPTER 15

Gaea

I can't believe I'm minutes away from saying *I do* to Kwame. After the way things ended the last time we were together, I never thought this would be possible. That shit was bad. If I'm being completely honest, shit was going bad because we had too many hands in our pot. The proof of that was our daughter being snatched and the reason I am currently laying in this bed with a bullet wound right under my left lung. To say I'm lucky to be alive is such an understatement because I'm honestly blessed to be here.

Waking up to see the face of a worried Kwame is beautiful. I never thought it would be him by my bedside, but I'm ecstatic that it is. I thought he had pushed me to the side and put that hoe Melody in my place. I wasn't really worried about her ass in the first place, because truth be told, I knew they would only last a season. A real threat to me wouldn't go out of her way to make her presence known. I won't lie and say I'm not mad or hurt, because I am. My efforts were being shit on! But today, I'll be walking into this brand-new life with Kwame. All of the sins of our lives together will be repented and washed away.

Thinking about how blessed I am brings me back to my happy place of singing. So I begin to sing the song weighing heavily on my heart.

She was lost in so many different ways,
Out in the darkness with no guide.
I know the cost of a losing hand,
But for the grace of God go. I, oh I,
I found heaven on earth.
You are my last, my first,
And then I hear this voice inside.
Ave Maria.

"I know you didn't think I was gonna let you marry that man with that ugly ass hospital gown on, did you?" Ana calls out, interrupting my impromptu song.

"Ana, it's not like I have anything here to wear. It will be quick and simple. I'll get to plan my wedding later," I say in a nonchalant way.

"Baby, nothing with Kwame will ever be quick and simple. This man has gone all out for you. He's been planning since the doctors came out and said you will be fine. The only time he left your side was when Kynsley had a fit about not having either one of her parents present. I know it's not ideal or traditional, but he has a gown for you," Ana states.

She then pulls out an ivory A-line vintage illusion dress. The backless spaghetti-strapped dress allows me to be sexy while still hiding my wounds. Looking at this dress allows me to see how much thought he put into making this special for me. With tears in my eyes, I allow Jenn and Ana to get me dressed. My hair is a giant task. Although it looks as if someone, I'm assuming Kwame, attempted to tame this beast, I need Jenn to work her magic with those flat irons. About two hours after I am completely dressed, my father comes in.

"Butterfly, since the day you were born, I swore I would protect you at all cost. I knew that if anything would happen to you, I would lay my heart down on the line to ease your pain, but it seems as if I failed to protect you from someone that should've been fighting right beside me to keep you safe."

"Daddy, don't. None of this is your fault. She fooled us all. The best part of all of this is that you and I can work toward healing our family together. If nothing else, we must hold on to the assurance that God holds us in His grace, and although this road has definitely been rough, He has saved his very best for us. His pure love and salvation is waiting for us on the other side. You are human, and oftentimes, humans fail. You are looking at living proof that life can somehow issue us a bad hand. But through prayer, love, and perseverance, we can get through it. *Together.* Dry your eyes, Daddy. You have done nothing but love your family, as you should have."

"Baby, Flash is such a lucky man. Your strength in all of this is inspiring. Kwame's strength to hold it all together lets me know that this is the man I would have hand-picked for you," he says as he holds my hand to walk me toward the chapel.

After a short walk, we are standing in from of the chapel doors. I take a deep breath and look at my dad, giving him the OK to open the doors. The doors open, and I am speechless. Kwame has filled the sanctuary with sunflowers and pink calla lilies. The significance of the two aren't lost on me. The pink calla lily symbolizes admiration and appreciation, whereas the sunflower symbolizes adoration, loyalty, and longevity. He's sending a message straight to my heart. This thing between us will be forever; it'll be whatever we make it. No longer will we be victims of our circumstances. We're coming out of this victorious. Anything that blocks the blessing that is us, has to be cut off. As I walk down the aisle, Brian McKnight caresses my ears.

First time I look into your eyes,
I saw heaven-oh-heaven in your eyes.
Everything I did before you
Wasn't worth my time.
It should have been you,

.

I told myself if Kwame isn't crying when I make my way toward him, I'm going to turn my ass back around and try this shit again until we get it right. We've spent too long trying to get to this point in life for him not to appreciate what a blessing it is. I get the surprise of my life when not only was he crying, but he's also the one that's singing and walking towards me. Who knew that this negro could hold a half a note? If I weren't so sore, I swear I would set this pussy on a platter for him. Nonetheless, he continues to serenade me as we make our way to Pastor Scott.

Here in these arms of mine,
The irreplaceable love of my life.

"Mommy, you look so beautiful. Just like a princess but only you're a mommy!" Kynsley says while hugging my leg tightly. As she stands before me in her flower girl dress, I have never felt prouder. Her journey to healing has taken us all through the ringer, but her smile and her will to persevere have kept us all from crumbling. She lets go of my leg and stands in between us, letting us know that this is her moment as well. I hand my bouquet to Ana grasp my daughter's hand and mentally go over my vows in my head. Although spur of the moment, I know what I need to say to Kwame.

"Kwame Langston, I've loved you as my friend since our first group project in our African American studies class. When you schooled me on what it's like to be an African American male in America. Since then, you've educated and informed me of a lot, always using a gentle hand with me and correcting me when I'm wrong. Oftentimes, I wasn't appreciative of your efforts, and we lost a lot of time because of my stubbornness. I realize now the error of my ways. All this time, I've been fighting a love that God has designed just for me. Through you, I found the love of God, and then it all clicked for me. Colossians 3:14 reads: And above all these, put on love, which binds everything together in perfect harmony."

"Baby, you are that love that made my darkest days better. You were the quiet strength that brought our daughter back to us and probably the reason I'm standing before you today. Here in front of our peers and the people that we love, I'm giving up my fight. I am yours from the soul out. I vow to be your peace. I vow to be your strength and to love you unapologetically," I declare as I wash away the tears that are on his face "Have a seat for me, baby," I say as I kneel before him and take the wash basin and wash towel from Jenn. After he is seated, I unlace his shoes and proceeded to wash his feet before I begin to speak again.

"Kwame, Jesus did this with his disciples as a symbol of his devotion to humble himself as a leader and serve his followers. I am doing this in complete surrender of my masculine ways. The stubborn part, we will have to work on a bit." I chuckle. "The significance of this for us is that from this day forward, as your wife, I am vowing to love you, trust your judgment, and ultimately let you take the lead role."

After drying his eyes, he asked everyone in attendance if they're recording this moment. Kwame boohoos through his vows and speaks on how God kept leading him to me. He speaks of how my fight and his decision to give up on our relationship broke us both down until God made us both sit down and take heed to where he was trying to take us. After saying I do, we looked over to see our daughter looking upset.

"What's wrong, Bumblebee?" I ask.

"Daddy gave you a ring, but I gots nothing!" She pouted.

"Baby, Daddy didn't forget you," he says as he puts a ring in the shape of a crown on her little fingers.

"Yay! I do three!" she says, jumping into his arms.

CHAPTER 16

Ana

*A*s cute as I find Kwame and Gaea to be is about as much as I find those muthafuckas to be annoying. I've never known two individuals who loved each other go through the dumbest shit. First, the love for each other foresees a future together, then the other person does some stupid ass shit, and then they are done with each other, sitting around looking ugly. Now that they are married, hopefully we don't have to deal with that shit anymore. But knowing them, we'll all be dragged into that shit. By all, I mean Tobias. I'm blocking all their asses for a month, especially Tobias. His real rude, real nosy ass has me feeling things I never wanted to feel. We're getting entirely too close. It's time for me to cut his ass loose. On some for real shit, he's fucking up my pimping. We're always together or fixing shit for my sister, so I haven't had time to get my shit together and truly get back to the things I enjoy doing—men.

It still doesn't change the fact that we're currently walking around the mall to find me some new panties. It's things like this that make me want to change the dynamics of our relationship. We walk for a bit until we make it to a small, very sexy lingerie shop, one that left nothing to the imagination. The entire store hits you from all angles, tickling all of your senses. It smells of sandalwood and vanilla, fully arousing me. The sound of Janet's "Would You Mind" caresses my ears. I'm starting to think it was a bad idea to bring Tobias into this store. But he eagerly follows me throughout this store.

He ventures out on his own, picking out a couple of different items that peak his interest and looking confusedly at others. It was hilarious watching him play around in the store. After finding a few items that compliment my physique best, I walk into the dressing room to begin trying things on, leaving Tobias out on the floor in a room full of aphrodisiacs. I know leaving him out there is bad when I receive a text from him.

Steeze: I must look like a total perverted Poindexter standing in this damn store waiting on you.

Why wait when you can come join me?

After sending that, I quickly snap a picture of me in next to nothing and giggle when I hear him mutter, "Goddamn." Soon there-after, I step out of the dressing room, wearing a very revealing, very sexy bra with my ass looking good enough to eat in the Kaylie Thong from Agent Provocateur. Tobias's eyes darken as he blurts out, "Turn around, let's see how that ass looks from all angles."

Like the naughty woman I am, I'm happy to oblige. I love showing off for him, reveling in his lustful stare. He knows how to appreciate my body and make me feel like I'm the only girl on the planet. It's in these moments that I crave all of the dysfunction that Gaea and Kwame have, but unfortunately, I can never have that.

"Great," Tobias finally declares. "Might even be as sexy as when you wear your compression shorts and when yo' hair is all over yo' fucking head."

"Thanks, I think," I respond as I do a little twerk, bringing his eyes right to my fat ass. "You know what? Just come back in the dressing room. I got some shit I want to show you. Then I won't have to parade around out here letting the world see all my goodies."

"What you trying to do, Boop? I don't think you really ready for this." Tobias chuckles. I answer by taking his hand, pulling his face down, and tongue fucking his mouth. I wait until I hear him moan before I lead him into the fitting room.

Alone together in the dressing room, I lick my lips and remove the bra I have been wearing, moving along with trying to decide what to try on next.

"You think I'll get some play in something like this one?" I ask Tobias, holding one up for him to see. But Tobias is too busy grabbing his dick and staring at my bare titties to notice anything I've said.

"I don't know, but I really like those two," Tobias says.

"Quit playing so much, man," I say with a giggle. "All I need from you in this moment is to give me your opinion of 'these two' in this one," I say as I pull on the bra in question. "Looks good," he says. "But let's see what this shit really can do."

With that, Tobias reaches out to gently pull my left tit out, gently pinching my nipple then licking it to ease the pain he causes. "OK, it is made with *fine material*." And finally, he reaches back to expertly unhook the bra with one hand and allow it to drop to the floor. Standing topless in front of him, I can't help but laugh. "You are too much," I coo out.

"Nah, that's yo' ass," he answers, gently kissing my forehead then trailing his tongue lightly down my face, my neck, to the tops of my breast, then around my nipple. "Yo, T, we can't do this in here," I say, but Tobias ignores my pleas and is now flickering his tongue across my nipple in quick succession, bringing his hand up gently to caress my engorged bud, which has been buzzing since we stepped foot into the store.

But now that Tobias is running his fingers up and down my velvety folds, the fact still remains I don't want to do this. Not right now anyway. We'll get too fucking loud in here. He'll just have to wait. I for damn sure am not about to censor myself of my nut for the sake of anyone else. I'm selfish when it comes to that. I'll fist fight Satan himself if he interrupts my moment. It's when I feel the most at peace. After a moment, I pull his head away and cup his face in my hands.

"Steeze, I'm not about to fuck you in this dressing room. OK?"

"Yeah, OK."

Taking the heat out of the moment, he brings the focus back to me and my recent behavior. I didn't mean to beat Janet's ass; that shit just fucking happened. If I'm being completely honest here, I should've beat her ass a long fucking time ago. She's just to disrespectful. She has been doing shit to me and Gaea for years and getting away with it because my daddy loved her. He can give her love. I, on the other hand, will be delivering fades left and right. For this last stunt, every time I see her, I'm dropping everything and beating her ass. I don't give a fuck if we're at her funeral. I'm dumping her ass out, beating her corpse, and stomping her ass an additional eight feet. It's just some shit you don't do, and setting your child up for whatever reason—whether it be financial or hate—is one of them. My daddy told me to be cool, but I can't sit back and cook when this bitch is feigning innocence. Nah, they could miss me with that.

That damn Melody tried that fuck shit too. I don't give a fuck what she thought she was to Kwame, but showing up during a crisis wasn't warranted. She could've sent a fucking text, an email, a smoke signal, or something before showing up. Especially since the hoe went on a whole tirade on social media about my sister wrecking her happiness. Nobody even knows Kwame was fucking with her for real, for real, because he never mentioned, followed, or friended her on anything. She would try to post pictures, but he quickly shut that shit all the way the fuck down with a few cease and desist orders. If that wasn't her clue that man didn't want her, then I don't know what is. Like, bitch, come on. You can't be that fucking stupid.

"Boop! You can't be wilding out on people the way that you do. One day you're going to meet your match."

"I haven't met a bitch yet that can whoop my ass. When you meet her, tell that bitch I'm ready for that ass whooping! But let that hoe know I have no problem sliding her ass straight to God!"

Tobias shakes his head and looks through more of the lingerie I've brought into the dressing room. Then he holds up a sheer teddy. "Why don't you try this on?" he suggests.

"Sure, why not," I say as I slip it over my head. It feels good, rubbing against my breasts. The evidence of the way it makes me feel were erect nipples.

He studies me for a moment, then says, "Yeah, it's OK. Of course, you wouldn't be wearing pants. Right?" I'm, for all intents and purposes, completely naked now in front of Tobias, frankly beginning to get really turned on by the situation as I feel the moisture seeping from my pussy.

Tobias licks his lips and adjusts his dick in his pants.

"Having a little trouble there, Steeze?" I ask him.

"Nothing I can't and will be willing to handle," he replies while slapping me on the ass.

"Well, how about if I handle it for you?" I ask as I push my hands down into his pants. I push his pants partially down and rub his dick to life. As I slowly stroke him, I lick the head of his beautiful dick. "I take it you like how my ass looks in this thing?"

"Oh yeah, you know I do. Stop playing with my shit if you not going to let me put this dick all off in you, Boop!" he growls. "What happened to 'I'm not into the fucking you in public thing'?" Tobias asks.

I don't even bother to answer. I'm more concerned with having his dick down my throat. Tobias has a beautiful dick, and I love watching that shit disappear down my throat, and the way that muthafucka would twitch two times before coating my throat with his seeds is orgasmic. I pull his pants down in one swift motion, reaching into his underwear to get my hand around his hard dick. I take his dick and try to swallow that shit whole. I'm bobbing my head, licking and slurping, getting real sloppy like he likes it. I run my tongue up his length while gently massaging his balls.

He responds by gripping a handful of my hair with one hand and reaching under the flimsy negligee with the other to find that my pussy was already wet. He dips a finger into my honeypot then spreads the wetness up to my clit. He continues teasing my aching vagina, letting his middle finger circle me for a moment, then he slides back down into her canal. Both of us are extremely turned on by now, eyes closed, breathing getting ragged.

"Do you need a hand in there?" It's the salesgirl outside the door, checking up on me. Tobias stops his ministrations while I continue to stroke him for dear life before responding.

"Um, no, thanks." While flicking my tongue over his mushroomed head, I mutter, "Everything I need is right here," I reply before I continued to deep throat him.

"OK," says the salesgirl. "I've got another customer on the floor, but I'll be back in a couple minutes. I have something else for you to try."

"All right. That was close," Tobias says. "I guess we'll pick this up when we get to my house."

"Yo, my dude, are you crazy? No way am I waiting to get my nut that long! I want it now. Right now. Let me just get you wet right now," I say as I turn around and ease his dick right in my treasure. The animalistic growl that emits from deep within his throat throws me into overdrive. I start a slow bounce, tightening my vagina muscles each time I bounce down on him. He grips my hips and starts to fuck me back. Each bounce is met with a slap on my ass until I cum.

I'm wearing just the negligee when he flips me over and pins me against the wall. He sinks right into me while strumming my clit. Sensing I'm about to get loud, he starts kissing me like I'm the last woman on this earth. The deeper he digs, the slower the kiss. If I'm not mistaken, Tobias is making love to not only my body but to my mind and heart. My heart is swelling, and I have to admit that I'm falling for my best friend, but that can't happen. Tobias is the closest thing I have to sanity, and I'm not willing to give that up. Like, not at fucking all.

I try to stop the kiss and push him away before we go too far— further than we've already gone. Tobias looks at me, knowing I'm retreating from the moment. He licks his lips and drops to his knees, bringing his sexy ass face to face with my pussy. He licks me from my ass to my clit before slipping his tongue in my ass and sucking the objection right out of my mouth. As he licks and flattens his tongue, the what if's in my head fade, and I'm solely focused on riding the wave and him sucking my soul right out of my body. In one swift movement, he squats down a bit to allow me to line up with the engorged mushroom head of his dick with my pussy hole. I hold my breath then push down while he pumps up, his dick sliding in effortlessly.

"Ohhhh," we moan in unison as I squeeze down on what's now becoming my dick.

"God, that feels so good. Tell me that this pussy is mine," Tobias growls in my ear. "If you keep clenching your pussy muscles like you are, I'm sorry, but this isn't going to take long."

"I don't want it to," I moan, overwhelmed by the instrument of pleasure splitting me open and the feelings floating around my heart. I pull my legs up around his neck, creating a deeper angle, letting him support me against the wall. Holding me tightly in his arms with my hands securely on the wall, he begins to fuck me like I want, delivering a clear message to me that this has gone far beyond our friendship and into dangerous territory.

The more he pounds in and out of me, the further I fall for him. This is a new position for us and far too intimate for me, so it takes a moment to find a good rhythm. But soon, we're in sync as Tobias's dick pushes in and out of my treasure chest of love. Our pelvises are mashed together in this position, resulting in lots of pushing and pulling and rubbing of my clit, which is driving me wild. Opening my eyes, I realize my freaky ass can watch the way we make love in the mirror behind us. And what a sight it is; that shit is beautiful, seeing his bare ass pulling back and pushing forward into me.

The sight brings me to another level of excitement. It's pushing past the moment and pushing me into a forever. Only I'm certain Tobias won't be able to love me fully when he discovers why I am the way I am. Surely, once he finds out, he'll be done with me. So I guess I need to live truly in this moment then store it for safekeeping because it won't happen again.

"Oh, God, I'm so close already," I moan. "Just a little more, a little more. Fuck me like you mean it, Tobias! Harder, babe! Harder!"

Tobias is struggling not to cum until I clench my walls as he strokes my pussy for dear life. As soon as I do that, he explodes, shooting his seeds deep into my pussy. He'd better pray that Plan B that I'm gonna take works. I feel waves of pleasure washing up into my core and down through my thighs. It takes us a good little bit before we're able to speak again. We're completely spent, hot, sweaty, and currently mashed up against each other in the small dressing room. Once catching our breath, we look deep into each other's eyes and then just start laughing. We can't believe what we've actually done.

Carefully disentangling ourselves, Tobias crams his barely softened dick back into his underwear and pulls up his pants. I quickly redress, avoiding contact, afraid that if I look at him again, I'll be fucking the life out of him, safely snatching his soul. Just as I finish zipping my pants, the annoying ass sales associate is back, knocking at the door. I open it, and she's holding out another negligee and saying, "I thought you might like to try this teddy."

"No thanks. Teddy's aren't really my thing," I mutter, clearly embarrassed because from the look on her face, I can tell she heard us. My ringing phone saves me from holding an awkward conversation. I grab the one I was wearing while Tobias fucked the shit out of me and signal I'm ready to purchase.

"Hello?"

"Hey, Butterfly, what's up?"

"Nothing, I was calling in a favor. Daddy isn't answering me or Kwame's calls. I'm worried, sooooo I was wondering if you can you do your little pop-up thing and see what's going on with him?"

"First off, that sounded like a whole run-on sentence. Why would I do that? I'm sure he just needs some privacy," I say, confused as to why she can't do this invasive shit herself.

"He listens to you. You and Tobias are good at being nosy. I'll meet you there shortly! Bye," she says before she hangs up in my face.

CHAPTER 17

Kwame

The decision to marry Gaea seemed so spur of the moment and for the most part it was. I just knew that I couldn't wait another moment to have her permanently in my life. I was letting my emotions lead me. Acting on a feeling and securing a life for my girls and I. We had no choice but to be great we had been through enough hell that we just had to see some sunshine from here. Following the wedding Gaea was released from the hospital and we had been camped out in our home. She was under strict orders to take it easy so I was doing everything in my power to make sure she didn't have to lift a finger.

Marriage didn't really change much for us, it just solidified that we were done playing games and that we were fully committed to each other. Unlike last time I leaked our marriage certificate before anyone else could make a mockery of our shit. I figured it was best to get ahead of the press so that I could jump back into practice and focus solely on that and my family during this up. As I sat and looked at the Instagram pics she posted of our daughter holding both of our left hands over her heart, I couldn't help but to feel a sense of peace. But that was short lived because my buzzing phone alerted me that I had an unwanted text.

Madd ass Mel: Flash, I was just texting to tell you congratulations. You have successfully entered the fuck boy status and played yourself. Just last week you were all in my space fucking me but this week you're married. Get the fuck out of here my man. I'll see to it that your precious little Gaea finds out where you lay your head when you're not with her.

I got six words for you Melody: You will be hearing from my lawyer Melody!

Madd Ass Mel: Let me say this just so that we are clear on a few things. 1. Courts don't fucking scare me 2. Wack ass Tobias is no threat to me. Try again nigga *laughing emoji* You will be hearing from me.

Instead of continuing to arguing with this psycho babe, I call up Tobias to put our plan in motion to shut her ass up for good. She may have though that she moved silently, but after her blow up at the hospital I knew to expect something from her ass. I just didn't know what. I mean I knew I was wrong for leading her own when my heart wasn't available in that capacity but I also knew it wasn't possible for her to love me like she proclaimed.

"Yo T, what are you up to?"

"Nothing much about to head into this court room and handle some business. What you need?" he asked noncommittedly

"Well I won't keep you long I need you to handle that slight work with that crazy ass broad." I rush out

"If you would've listened to me in the first place, we wouldn't have to be shit. Make this the last time have to do some dumb ass shit like this. I didn't go to school to do no dumb ass shit like this man!" I barked out

"Man chill out. I'm good with Gaea. But I do need to know the extent of the relationship between her and that nigga Drexel."

"If she ain't checking into crazy ass Melody then let sleeping dogs lie. If they said it wasn't shit, there then it ain't shit there. I don't know about the next man but what good would it do to lie on yo dick? Let

99

that shit go and go love on your wife and daughter. I'll holler at you later" He said disconnecting the call before I could say bye.

He had a point, if I was truly taking this marriage with Gaea serious then I needed to let go of this lingering insecurity. I truly was tripping because of the shit I was currently going through with Melody. But I was going to make sure that his ass didn't pop up like an unwanted case of herpes.

CHAPTER 18

Melody

$\mathcal{I}$ don't know who Flash thinks he's playing with, but I'm not the fucking one. He should've never looked my way the day we met. Truth of the matter is it was no coincidence that we met. The shit wasn't kismet or anything like that; it was strategically planned, though falling in love with him was accidental. I honestly didn't think the shit was possible, but he made it so fucking easy. He was everything I desired in a man. He provided the stability in a man I needed, especially since my daddy couldn't be that.

The woman that he loved so much broke his heart. When he discovered her love and greed for money, it meant more to her than we did. So here I am at twenty-eight, going completely undercover, risking my job to follow a lead to find her. At first, the lead seemed fruitless until I stumbled across a dance studio. Creative Expressions proved to be the thread that was going to burst this case wide open for me. Only it wasn't as easy to get close to the owner, so I set my sights on her sister. Well, rather our sister—Gaea. Yeah, you guessed it. I am the long forgotten older sister of the two Lee sisters. Janet Lee is my mother, but only by blood. This bitch is by means nobody's anything.

The life I thought I was missing out on seemed to be bullshit compared to what I have with my daddy. I may have had to strip to make ends meet in undergrad, may have had to beg for better clothing, and had to do without on a lot of things, but I guess I should consider myself blessed. My father did the best he could as a single father to make sure that I wanted for nothing. But I did want for things.

I wanted a mother who halfway gave a damn about me. When I found out that I had sisters, that shit enraged me. How were they good enough to keep, but I was tossed to the side like I wasn't shit? She made the conscious decision to keep them but made no effort to make sure I was safe. I, Melody Alaina, was a nobody in her world of somebodies.

I never realized how much this shit affected me and my threshold for trust and love until my boyfriend of five years left me. He was tired of me always accusing him of shit that I literally concocted in my head, never mind the fact that he was *always* present. His final straw was finding out that I didn't trust his ability to lead me after the birth of our son. I would disengage and push them both away. He accused me of being exactly like my mother and walked away with our son. I didn't doubt it. I knew that I needed to heal prior to attempting to be in my son's life. Hence me implanting myself into my sisters' lives.

I try to put into words what a breach of trust feels like. But I can't conjure up the words that'll paint the reality of how it makes me feel. It ultimately boils down to security and stability. If I don't feel stable or lack that security, I flee and move to the next station of what I find conducive to the peace I try to speak on daily. Sometimes, closure isn't needed to bring you that peace. Root removal is. By removing the root, you're eliminating the source of pain and not allowing its toxic vibe to infect other areas of your life. In this case, root removal is just what the doctor ordered in my need to get better so that I can be a better woman for my son. All it boils down to is that Janet has to go. Period! In order for me to find peace in my life, I have to face and get rid of the bitch who scarred me. Thirty years of this shit is enough.

My father told me even if I were to find Janet, I'll never get the answers I need to heal, because she isn't sorry for breaking me. I get what he was getting at, but I want to hear her say that to my face. Through therapy, what I've truly learned is that people are only able to break you when you allow them to do so. Am I blaming myself for Janet's transgressions? No. I just need to find a balance to get to an OK point in life. Finding that balance between love of self and love of the world and its people to nurture your own heart is key. As I continue on this journey to healing, I look back on 2 Timothy 1:7 in times I feel I need to re-center myself. It reads: For the Spirit God gave us does not make us timid, but gives us power, love, and self-discipline.

I know that hurt is inevitable, but continuing to go down the path of hurt or carrying that hurt with you isn't conducive to taking care of you. I can't love myself or my own child, because I'm searching for a love that I'll never get from Janet. My therapist told me to grow from my breach of trust and don't allow it to change me. I literally have to let go of all of the pain and continue to follow my God-given light. The actions of others shouldn't hinder me; I've found that Janet is continuing to live her shady ass life, while I'm trapped in self purgatory. It isn't fair to me at all.

I remember that Satan is tricky and a whole heap of trifling. Lucifer can sometimes deliver things in the form of a blessing as well. Take a minute stop and reread that last line once again. Sometimes, the devil will take what you desire most and wrap that turmoil and dysfunction up so pretty that it can quickly be mistaken for a blessing. Like who but Satan can make pain look identical to a blessing? The problem with him and his trickery is you won't be able to recognize it until it is too late.

My too late point was Flash. I don't know what I was thinking when going into that hospital, but I needed to be there. I just wanted Janet to see my face and to admit to everyone what a terrible mistake she's made in giving me up. Only I didn't count on my sister to beat my ass. Anais beat my ass so good that I was stuck in this damn apartment for the last week, nursing my wounds. She even checked Flash. If it was any other time, I would've shook her hand and given her props.

Being a woman who is no stranger to his tricks and who has definitely been on a journey because of these tricks, I understand the pain wrapped inside of them. I'm stating blatantly the journey was not a pretty one. I've hit rock bottom once or twice in my life, chasing disguised blessings. I won't lie and say that the journey wasn't fun, because in most cases, it was indeed fun. But that hellish aftermath. Oh my Lord, was it awful. Liquor nor tears can repair that heartache. I mean, not that liquor was my vice. It's just a colloquialism of sorts. But you catch my drift. *Nothing* I tried would get me through it. Probably because the prayers were being answered, but it just wasn't an answer I wanted to hear.

In order to get over this hurdle, I, at first, need to reevaluate the desires of my heart and see where I can find my very own fault in the midst of that storm. You see, if I'm not open to self-doubt, insecurity, vulnerability, and fear, I wouldn't have been where I once was. The devil's job isn't to bring me peace and happiness, no, it's quite the opposite. The more miserable I am, the happier he then becomes. His job is to assure that I'm free falling willingly into his home of doom.

Once you open your spirit up to ugliness and gloom, there they would dwell and make a chaotic home. You only have two options: fix the negative connotations of your desire or allow the devil to fester and make you miserable. You have to allow the will of God to move throughout your life and manifest the beautiful blessings. You have to get out of your own way and put in work to rejoice in your blessings. *"Faith without work is dead."*

"Melody. Thanks for meeting me here. I don't know what your aim is with Kwame, but I assure you that whatever the case may be, your plans will never succeed. So what's your aim?"

"Not that it is any of your business, but I happen to be very much in love with Flash," I state, unmoved by his overpowering presence. I've been in the trenches with niggas bigger than him.

"Look, Melody, we both know that is a flat-out lie. You can save that loud talking, lying shit for ya mammy. It's evident you don't know this man, for if you did, you wouldn't be calling him Flash! So again, I ask, what do you want with Kwame?" Tobias asks.

"Look, you may be able to intimidate the rest of these spineless ass people, but you don't put an ounce of fear in my heart, my nigga. I walked through the trenches to get to where I am today, so again, your presence doesn't move me."

"OK, bitch, since you want to talk reckless, let me make this shit plain for you. Here is a gag order forbidding you to speak on anything involving Kwame Langston Jacobsen. You should've been upfront about your shit and what you really wanted, but you wanted to play tough. Let's see if yo' duck ass can get close to Janet now," he says as he stands to leave.

"Wait! How did you know?"

"I know everything when it boils down to the people I love. Granted, I don't fuck with Janet, I'm well aware what goes on in her life."

"Look, all you need to know is the shit with her has nothing to do with ya bum ass friends. This shit with Janet is very fucking personal. What I need you to remember when you fucking with a bitch like me is you don't move me with your idle threats! I've been through the trenches and have had my ass whooped more than a few times, but that shit pushed me to not fold or break. So you see this cease and desist and that wack ass gag order y'all issued are just drops in the bucket on the grand scale of things. Being nosy is a female trait, Tobias. Get you some business that doesn't involve mine!"

"Bitch, you think Ana whooped yo' ass before. Imagine what it is gonna be like once she realizes that not only did you try to fuck her sister's husband, but you were using all of them to get close to Janet, who just so happens to be your mother!" he growls before walking out of the restaurant. I sit for a moment, contemplating my next move until I see Janet and a woman arguing. I know then that this is my chance, so I pay my tab and follow her out.

CHAPTER 19

Theodore

*I*f you would've told me a year ago, hell, even one day ago that my wife would turn out to be the one to put any of my girls in danger, I would call you a liar. Sure, I knew she wasn't innocent; she has been raising hell in their lives, but I attributed it to growing pains. I knew from living in the home with my own mother and sister how exasperating that can be, but I never for one moment thought we would be here. I've been sitting in my office for the last couple of hours, trying to figure this shit out, but I'm coming up blank.

As I throw the last of my Bourbon down my throat, my oldest baby girl, Anais, comes waltzing through my door. She's so beautiful, but that beauty is hidden by the tough exterior she puts on to face the world. Ana is my firecracker. If anything, I can count on her shenanigans to ease my pain. But as of late, she's been hiding them too, and I can never get to the bottom of it with all of the shit that's unraveling before me. But I will.

"Hey, Daddy! Why haven't you been answering my calls?" she asks.

"Hey, Punkin. I didn't hear it ring. What brings you by?" I ask, already knowing the answer to the question. She may be tough, but by nature, my baby's a protector. She's shown and proven that to us time and time again when it comes down to Gaea and me.

"Daddy, did you seriously ask me why I'm stopping by? You know why I'm here. Do you want me to help you pack things up?" she asks, serious as all hell. I knew I would have to face someone in regard to what I've decided to do. Separation and divorce are hard things to deal with, but magnify that by one million when you have millions of dollars involved. Do I love Janet? Sure. But I love my money and my girls more. If I could figure out a way to get rid of her ass without losing either, I would. I just have to be careful when it comes down to dealing with her. A scorned woman is a dangerous woman.

"Punkin, let's not jump the gun here. I have to think strategically. Although heartless, your mother is not a stupid woman," I say.

"Daddy, say the word, and I will beat her muthafucking ass! You saved her ass twice now; it won't be a third," she says, never looking up from her phone. "My bad, Daddy. I didn't mean to curse, but know that I'm high-key serious. But ummm... you and Gaea have to figure out how to deal with your shi-stuff because this no showering thing is flat-out nasty. Go get in the shower while I go and whip you up a meal because I know you haven't eaten."

"Sometimes, I wonder who raised you because that mouth is awful," I say, chuckling but heading out of my office to shower.

After handling my business, I hate to admit it, but Ana is right. I do feel a little better, but coming down to the kitchen to the sound of laughter has me on edge. The last time I heard laughter of this sort was the day that Gaea and Kwame decided they could no longer do life alone. I'm genuinely happy for them. If I'm being honest, I have rooted for them since the day I found out that Kwame was Kynsley's father. I looked deep into his life and figured when the time was right, they would get their shit together. That fact was only solidified once we joined forces to find Kynsley.

As I stepped into the kitchen, my confusion died down when I realized I had both of my baby girls here with me.

"Hey, baby girl, how are you feeling?" I ask while kissing her on the forehead.

"Hey, Daddy. I'm doing well. I just convinced Kwame to get me out of the house for a spell so that I can check on you. Before you ask, he's in the sitting room with T and Kynsley," she replies just as the doorbell rings.

"I got it!" Ana calls as she makes her way toward the front door.

"Where is Theodore? Theo, bring your stupid ass out here! I got some shit to say to you, and you're going to fucking listen to me!"

"Maxine, I know like fucking hell you did not just barge yo' raggedy ass up in my Daddy house acting like a whole hood possum!" I hear Ana say as she blocks her way to further enter the house.

"Maxine, stop. If you do this, I'll never forgive you!" Janet runs up behind her saying.

"Fuck forgiveness, bitch! You weren't thinking about forgiveness while you were fucking me, my husband, and yours! Bitch, you're trash! You better be lucky I love you too much to kill you!"

Before I have the opportunity to align my mind with my actions, I have my hands around Janet's throat, choking the life out of her. This bitch has me so fucked on so many levels. I knew she was moving funny; I just never thought this bitch was putting my life at risk by fucking all these damn people. The shit hurt because like I said before, I loved her ass with everything I had in me to give. She's going to pay for the amount of pain she's put me through.

"Daddy, it's not worth it. Let me handle her!" Anais says while tugging my arm to get me off of Janet.

"Everybody, get the fuck up and head to the living room!" a voice yells.

"Jeffery, what the fuck are you doing here!" I yell while charging toward him.

"I'm just getting what is owed to me!" he says before a gun goes off.

"Noooooo!" is all I hear before everything goes black.

TO BE CONTINUED...

ONE MORE THING...

Hey Love!

It's me again. I know it took me a minute to get this second install-
ment out, but I wanted to make sure it wasn't rushed and that
everyone that needed to say something got it out. Though it may not
be what you wanted them to say, understand their stories aren't
complete. As soon as I finished this, I picked my pen back up to start
their finale. It won't be my next novel, so bear with me. I'm promising
to have it done prayerfully by mid-July. If you're my friend on social
media, remind me of said deadline. But in the meantime, check out
the first chapter of Anais's story.

Britt Joni

.

-PENNING LOVE NATURALLY-

WHAT'S NEXT FOR THE LEE SISTERS?

YOUR LOVE IS MY LIFELINE

SNEAK PEEK

Anais

The very thing many people proclaimed they wanted most was the very thing I couldn't give a half a fuck about. Love. Who needed that shit? I mean, honestly, who was sane enough to seek out that feeling? Tsk. The best feeling for me was an orgasm. It drowned out the noise, it silenced the violence, and it blacked out all of the emotions I was choosing to ignore. Horrific nightmares and a lifelong scarlet letter was what love got me. So I used those orgasms to empty myself. I emptied myself so that I could refill and refuel my soul with the things it needed to survive and not the cliché shit that most people said to please other people.

Nah... That's not my aim. This was about me. I was too busy putting shit I should've never said in a box, sorting out my emotions with my most recent ex, and boxing up old feelings with my friends of yesteryear. So what was I refilling and refueling my soul with, you ask? I refilled on souls. Soul ties to be specific. Sounded crazy, but it was toxic. But I needed their energy to keep me going. If it was bad energy, I'd purge that shit and keep it moving.

The souls I collected from men, I couldn't give two fucks about. I wasn't interested in their first or last names. All I craved was their testosterone in the same way they craved my yoni. I was a self-proclaimed man eater. That testosterone gave me the strength to keep going. I ate them strictly for their strength, and after the orgasm, I quickly replaced them with something more meaningful, you know like burning sage and a glass of sweet red or white wine.

I was the woman your mother warned you about. Lose, lost, and uncouth. I wasn't for everybody and never had been. But that wasn't any of my business, nor would it begin to be. That was strictly their own business. I wasn't pacifying anyone anymore. Pleasing the masses was a thing of the past unless it involved my dance studio. Now that was my heart but currently a frustration because, well, my dancers were fucking up.

"Point those feet! Ugly feet can be seen whether you're leading the front or carrying the back!" I huffed. I didn't know how many times I had to remind this class of elites that ugly feet were an eye sore. Too many to count; that's for damn sure. There was a reason my company was number one, and it wasn't because of ugly fucking feet.

"Start from the top. The next person I see with sloppy ass feet will be cut. I'm giving no more second chances! Competition is next week!" I barked at them, not giving a clear fuck about anyone's opinion.

Don't be mistaken by my foul mood; I loved these girls. Hell, I'd go to war for them, but they had to put in work because I saw the great-ness in them. I just needed them to see it and want it too. Since they were my babies, they knew my biggest pet peeve was sickled feet. Well, that and, you know, attachment, commitment, fuckboys, this new generation of what I had tagged as crack babies, and well, life.

If I was being completely honest with myself, I'd like to state on record that I wasn't in any means of the words happy. I was good at fronting. Hell, I'd been putting on a façade for damn near an entire decade. But that wasn't to say that I didn't have happy moments. I had happy moments, like spending time with my sister, Gaea and her family, especially my little niece, Kynsley.

The birth of my niece was one of my best moments in life. She was my entire heart outside of my body. The rest of my happiness was brought on by orgasms. That's probably why I chased them so much. Each orgasm brought me a little bit of peace. I couldn't really explain the why; all I could really explain was that I felt powerful and in control in those few minutes if that made any sense.

The only time I felt out of control was when I was being intimate with Tobias. As blissfully sweet as it may have been, I was definitely not trying to go down that road with him. T would make a lot of women in this world happy, and unfortunately, I couldn't be that girl. He was my friend. Albeit with benefits, he was just that, a friend. He bothered me though. He was nosy and had the tendency to see things that others often overlooked, things you wanted hidden, things that could possibly break you. But around these parts, I did the breaking these days, not the other way around.

My buzzing phone stole me away from my thoughts. I picked up the phone and opened my text thread.

*Steeze: Boop can we talk? *thinking emoji*.*

About what, Steeze?

I saw three dots appear and then disappear about three times before a text finally came through.

Steeze: About you... About us... About everything... Don't play coy Boop.

Nothing is wrong with me... We are cool. I'm a little busy though. I'll hit you back later on when shit slows down.

After sending that last text, I tossed my phone back into my bag. There was no reason to go down this road with Tobias to figure things out no matter how I felt for him. We were friends, and friends we would remain. We couldn't go any other route for any other reason other than I was in all essence of the word—toxic. Tobias's heart and soul were too pure, too open, too vulnerable, too valuable, and too nurturing for a woman like me to ruin. He would thank me one day for saving him from a wretch like me.

Feeling my frustrations mounting, I ended practice. It was only so many sickled feet, awkward lines, half ass leaps, and broken turns I could stomach. This was my baby, and I'd be damned if I let these girls half ass it. Needing a release and not wanting to find it horizontally, I stripped down to my leotards and began to stretch.

The musical musings of Me'shell Ndegeocello's "Faithful" filled the room with a beautifully somber melody. As she serenaded me, I said a quick prayer asking God to guide my steps and to keep my kinesthetic memory intact. I started off in second position and slowly started with soft, isolated movements. I broke from isolations and started slowly with pencil turns, breaking my body and contorting it to fall in sync with not only the song but my spirit as well.

My daddy made no excuse.
I believe my lies are truth.
Why won't you eat what you are fed?
When I touch myself, I think of only you.
And when I touch someone else.
No one is faithful. I am weak.
I go astray.
Forgive me for my ways.

As I leaped, twirled, and glided across the floor, I felt a dam break, so I danced harder and longer. The music became my purgatory, and I repeated this dance until I fell to the floor, completely exhausted and defeated. I wiped my face of the tears I unknowingly shed and took a minute to breathe. Sensing I wasn't going to get any kind of reprieve, I packed up my things and locked the doors to Creative Expressions.

I felt heavy in a way that I couldn't really explain. All I truly knew was that I needed a release and fast. I wanted to feel better—no, I needed to feel better, to not feel any of the emotions I was currently feeling. Disgust, hurt, regret, anger, and sorrow. Seeing the liquor store off to my right, I saw this as my chance to numb my feelings until another day. I made a quick turn and pulled in. I just wanted to drink until I couldn't feel anymore.

I parked and ignored the cat calls of the niggas outside of the store as I walked in. I may fuck, but I had standards, and fucking a nigga loitering outside of the liquor store wasn't something I was willing to do. But it never seemed to fail—some wack, stale-breath ass bastard was trying his luck. Today was no exception to that rule. I couldn't even get ten steps away from my car before a light-skinned, gray-eyed goblin of a man was wrapping his arms around my waist and invading my space. Before I could catch myself, I was snapping his wrist and kneeing him in the nuts.

"Don't ever fucking touch me without permission!" I barked.

"You fucking bitch! You broke my gotdamn hand. Mugsy, take me to the hospital!" he cried out while cradling his wrist. I sucked my teeth and continued into the liquor store. Once inside, I beelined straight in the direction of my favorite friends, Jack, Crown, D'USSÉ, and heavenly Hennessy.

"Shit!" I mumbled once I saw the heavenly melanin-coated African King standing amongst my friends. He stood at about six feet four with muscles that were beautifully tatted, big hands, juicy lips the color of burnt sienna, perfectly straight, white teeth, the most captivating hazel eyes, and dreads flowing down his back as if he were Samson himself. That muthafucka was fine! My Gawd was he fine. If I were wearing panties, a bitch would need to change them. I had to have been staring, because I heard a deep Barry White baritone pull me from me my thoughts.

"Say, Lil' Mama, you need help with anything?" he asked, flashing a panty-snatching smile. His ass wasn't as slick as he thought he was; I saw him give me a thorough look over before licking his lips.

So I did what any sexually liberated woman would do. I slid between him and bent over to pick up my babies for tonight. Once I was directly in front of him, I wiggled my ass on him then stood up. Bringing my face close to his, I cuffed his thick dick and responded, "Nah, boo, I got what I need."

Imagine my surprise when he lifted me up by my ass and brought his lips crashing down onto mine. I let out a sort of needy moan as he planted panty-wetting trails of kisses, nibbles, and licks along my neck. Liquor be damned, I was going to release these feelings in the form of a guaranteed orgasm. What he didn't know, I was willing to teach his ass tonight.

As dread head carried me into the back office, I felt him pull my leotard to the side and run his finger up my folds, getting them completely coated in my sweet nectar. This shit was just what the doctor ordered so that I could release the heaviness Tobias text had set on my shoulders. Why couldn't he just be OK with all that I had to offer? Friendship. Genuine friendship. I was too broken and toxic to be anything other than friends.

Dread head nibbling on my neck and sanity with each kiss brought me back into the here and now. He eased the top of the leotard down, pulling a caramel nipple into his mouth, flicking his tongue and biting down just a bit to keep me present in the moment. He began to lick and kiss his way down my body, sending a liquid heat to my treasure chest of love. Just as he planted a kiss to my sweet spot and suckled, I stopped him.

"You're not my man, boo. Do not put your lips on my forbidden fruit," I said, placing a finger under his chin.

"What's the difference, lil' mama? You letting a nigga fuck you, so why can't I suck the cum out of this sweet pussy?"

"Yo, you talking too much," I said while hopping off the desk and making quick work of pulling his pants down and rolling a condom on him. I stripped completely out of my dance attire, knowing that a visual of me bent over the desk would take the argument off of his lips. I busted it wide open and spread my cheeks to make it real for him. I took my finger, ran it along my slickened folds, and brought it to my mouth and sucked my finger.

"You really gonna turn all of this down because you can't have a taste?" I teased, putting on my best innocent girl act. That must have been just what he needed, because before I could sit up straight, he had already sunk deep inside of me. He'd pull out slowly and dive back in, teasing me and driving me crazy with lust. I felt my core heat, and I was off chasing that orgasm that I knew would help me feel better even if I was losing my dignity and if only for a moment in time.

As if he sensed I was close, he flipped me over, placing both legs on his shoulders and started fucking me like it was the best piece of pussy on this side of heaven. I mean, it was, but damn, this nigga would have me doubling back, and that was some shit I just didn't do.

117

"How this dick feel, mamas?" he breathed out into my neck.

"Less... talk... more... dick..." I barely got out breathlessly. Uttering those words spurred him on drowning me—well, rather us both, wave for wave into orgasmic bliss. Almost immediately after we were coming down from the bliss, the heaviness was back. I eased back into my leotard, daring him to speak. I just needed him to walk out as if nothing had happened and ring up my purchases so that I could get home to the comfort of my own bed and sulk. I didn't know why I continued to do this shit to myself, already knowing that the outcome would not be pretty. I had no one to blame for this but myself and, well, not facing my feelings for Tobias. To make matters worse, I let this nigga kiss me, and that was a huge no-no! Fucking Tobias, man!

"So will you be swinging back by next week?" Dread head asked.

"Look, Jared, I made the mistake in doubling back, but trust me when I say this. This"—I wave my hand between the two of us —"won't be happening again."

"Whatever you say, mamas," he said as he bagged up my liquor and ignored me trying to pay.

"Take the card, Jared. I fucked you because I wanted to, not for the fucking liquor," I spat out, still trying to pay.

"How about you just deduct the forty-five dollars from my goddaughter's dance dues this month, and we call it even," he said as I followed his eyes to the logo on the jacket that was now tied around my waist.

"Wait, you know who I am?"

He nodded, and I rolled my eyes, frustrated with the lack of self-control I had. I was shitting where I ate.

"Fuck! Yeah... This... Just, yeah, she can have next month free as long as you keep this shit between us."

"Your secret is safe with me, mamas," he said as I collected my loot and stormed out of the store.

My drive home was only a blur, but I managed to park my vehicle and make my way to the elevators. I said a quick hello to my door-man, Randy, and pressed the button to my floor to close the door to the elevator. I made the long trek to my door, fumbling with my keys to open the door. Once opened, I dropped my keys on the entryway table and began to strip out of my clothes, dropping them as I made my way to my guest bathroom to wash away all of my failures. I started the shower and walked out of the bathroom, giving the shower time to steam before I immersed myself in the serenity of the water-fall shower I recently had installed. I made my exit to make myself a drink. I mixed it just how I liked it—a splash of ginger ale and heavy on the Hennessey. One sip alone let me know that this wouldn't be enough. Feeling so disgusted with myself, I told Alexa to play The Weeknd's "Wicked Games."

Bring your love, baby, I could bring my shame.
Bring the drugs, baby, I could bring my pain.
I got my heart right here.
I got my scars right here.
Bring the cups, baby, I could bring the drink.
Bring your body, baby, I could bring you fame.
And that's my motherfuckin' words too.
Just let me motherfuckin' love you.

As the music flowed poetically through my speakers, I eyed a bottle of pain medication from a recent injury and poured them into my hand. I tossed them into my mouth and let the Hennessy chase them down my throat and ease them into my system. I told Alexa to keep that song on repeat before I stumbled back into the bathroom. I sat in the steam for a few minutes, reflecting on the last few months before I eased into the shower. I allowed the pain I'd felt for years to guide down my face, and before long, I was crying, screaming, and punching the wall before I collapsed, and everything faded to black. In those moments, I could no longer feel anything but peace.

ABOUT THE AUTHOR

Britt Joni is a Midwestern girl with Southern roots. She's a sucker for a good romance and gets giddy anytime there's a strong representation of black love. If asked to describe herself she'd probably tell you she is a modern day hippie with a dope soul. In short Britt Joni is a book hoarding, journal writing, Neo Soul & 90's R & B grooving, natural hair wearing, Chadwick Boseman loving, wine and whiskey consuming, kismet believing, lipstick junkie, who just wants to spread her love and gift of writing with someone other than herself. When Britt Joni is not chasing down her dreams with a pen, she is being a mommy to an AMAZING little boy.

Britt Joni has always used writing as a form of therapy. From a very early age she has always carried multiple journals around to jot down her thoughts, scribble down a quick poem, or to write out a story. After losing her biological father she decided life was too short to live in fear or with regrets so she took a leap of faith and started following her dream of writing. Britt Joni's ultimate literary goal is to write from the heart and to let her fascination with black love soar into the world.

Musical Inspiration for the novel:

http://bit.ly/TheSecretsWeKeep2

STAY CONNECTED
Twitter: @authorbrittjoni
Instagram: @authorbrittjoni
Facebook: Britt Joni and Author Britt Joni
Facebook reading group: Britt Joni's Oasis of Love

Website: www.brittjonipens.com
Email: authorbrittjoni@gmail.com

Be sure to LIKE our Major Key Publishing page on Facebook!

CPSIA information can be obtained
at www.ICGtesting.com
Printed in the USA
LVOW13s0756140718
583547LV00023BA/452/P